For all the queers

THE MINISTRY OF GUIDANCE

and Other Stories

Golnoosh Nour

MUSWELL
PRESS

First published by Muswell Press in 2020

Typeset by M Rules
Copyright © Golnoosh Nour 2020

Golnoosh Nour has asserted her right to be
identified as the author of this work in accordance
with the Copyright, Designs and Patents Act, 1988

Printed and bound by
CPI Group (UK) Ltd, Croydon CR0 4YY.

A CIP catalogue record for this book is
available from the British Library

ISBN: 9781916129283

Muswell Press
London N6 5HQ
www.muswell-press.co.uk

Contents

The Ministry of Guidance

S ogol entered her mother's bedroom and asked her if she had a chador.

Her mother closed her book and widened her honey-coloured eyes. 'Why?'

Sogol smiled, barely concealing her excitement. 'I've been given an appointment for the Ministry of Guidance tomorrow!'

'I know,' her mother said, 'but why do you want to wear a chador?'

'To fool them,' Sogol laughed, 'to look chaste!'

'Actually, I do have one,' her mother said, half-laughing, 'a proper black one I used to wear when I first started teaching.'

'See, I'm not the only hypocrite. I have to be sure that they'll grant permission for my poetry collection!'

Her mother opened the wooden door of her closet, stepped into it and rummaged through her sheets and clothes. 'I'm not sure if I can find it though,' she murmured. 'Oh, here it is!' Stepping out of the closet, she handed a lengthy black cloth to Sogol. 'Wear it now! You should look

1

confident and comfortable in it, otherwise, they'll know it's the first and last time you're wearing it.'

She dropped the chador over Sogol's head, and they both looked in the enormous wooden-framed mirror on the vanity table beside the bed. After a few seconds of surprise, they both let out a hysterical laugh. 'Actually, it kind of suits you,' Sogol's mother said, still laughing, 'you look like the actresses in the TV shows shown during Ramadan. Chaste. And fake.'

Sogol guffawed back, 'I'm not fake! I actually look like a proper Muslim girl. It has transformed my whole character; weird how one piece of clothing can do so much.'

Sogol let go of the chador and it fell to the floor. 'Thanks, Mum.' Staring into her mother's eyes, she thought about their strangely beautiful colour: *asali*.

Her mother touched her shoulders. 'Don't worry, your book will be published. We have already censored all the naughty things in your poems. They will pick on a few things, you will change them, and done. That's how it is with my translations. It's not difficult, just annoying.'

'I know. But I really want this, I've never wanted anything as much as the publication of this book. I want to become a real poet.'

'You are a real poet,' her mother reassured her.

'You know what I mean.'

When Sogol left her mother's bedroom at midnight, she realised she was shaking in ecstasy, holding in her hands the black chador, the key to her dreams.

Despite the fact that she had to get up early in the morning in order to make it to the Ministry of Culture and

Islamic Guidance at nine a.m., she couldn't fall asleep. She lay awake till three in the morning until she finally fell asleep, dreaming of strolling with her mother in green alleys, watching the sunset, and finally fathoming the colour of her mother's almond-shaped eyes – not the colour of honey, but sunset. And then she recalled that was an image in one of her poems, called 'Honey of the Sun', *asal-e-khorshid*.

She woke up at seven with The Fugees' 'Ready or Not' blasting out of her mobile, but she could not open her eyes because they were too dry. She got out of bed, eyes half-closed, head throbbing, her room the golden-orange of the sunset in her dream. She looked around her room and saw the chador lying furled on the floor, a dead serpent.

She went to the bathroom, cautious not to make any sound so her mother wouldn't wake up. While urinating, she imagined herself at the Ministry of Guidance. She was excited about going to that castle, thrilled about wearing a chador, acting chaste, pretending to be a virginal Muslim girl. Then she thought of all the boys and girls she wrote poetry about, and thought about her mother. She hadn't told her mother that the first page would be a dedication note to her. For everything she had done, for all the encouragement and inspiration. Sogol wanted to weep with a strange joy, despite the fact that it was early in the morning and she felt groggy. she realised she was sitting on the toilet seat for nothing, just thinking about being published and making her hard-working mother proud. She pulled up her pants and looked in the mirror while she brushed her teeth. Her toothbrush moving in and out of her mouth felt like congealed vomit. She wished she could eat something before leaving the house, but she knew she couldn't eat at such an early hour; she could

3

hardly open her mouth. She kept staring at her puffy, sleepy face in the mirror. Sogol knew everybody who considered her pretty did so only because they hadn't seen her mother. Everybody who saw her mother, only called her *naz*: cute, never pretty, and they were absolutely right.

She thought of her age, twenty-three, and her mother's, fifty-five, and thought the impossible thought. Sogol thought of her poem, 'Age'. 'Your age is raining on me, like cactus on bare skin'. What did she even mean? She almost hoped her poetry would get rejected because it was bad and publishing it would be a disgrace. But they were still poems. It would make her mother happy.

She went to her room, putting a black scarf on her head, *maghna'e*. The formal headscarf, something she used to wear at school and then at the university. Something she hated. A black scarf that would just fit the head, sewn under the chin. Covering the breasts and neck also. She then wore a long green *manteau* to look bad. Bad enough to be chaste. She looked in the mirror and realised she was happy. She avoided using any make-up to look even more chaste and innocent. She knew that, without it, her face looked like the face of a clueless twelve-year-old. She was aware she could look innocent even when she wasn't. This was all a game and she was going to win. Her mother knew people in the publishing industry, and she could go to the formidable Ministry only because her mother had pulled strings. She was, after all, lucky. Sogol put on a quilted black jacket on top of her *manteau* to keep warm. And then she threw the chador on her head, almost laughing in the mirror, suffocated by excitement. *If this is the price of being published, I will pay it: it will be funny.*

She left their house in Vanak, and walked to the main square in order to flag down a shared taxi. She didn't feel like driving through the morning traffic of Tehran. She wanted to snore happily in the *taksi* behind her enormous sunglasses, cut off from her surroundings; she just couldn't deal with the morning, the smoke, the people shouting about politics at eight a.m. Her eyes were aching from lack of sleep. She wanted to be home, and to find an excuse to enter her mother's bedroom and cuddle with her on the bed, under the pretext that it was cold.

She was aware that her friends and classmates were mostly applying to continue their studies abroad: the US, the UK, Canada, Germany, France, and even Malaysia. 'Anywhere but here. Studying is an excuse to leave,' her best friend, Yasaman, had said. But Sogol would never do that. She loved her country like a mother loving her mentally-disabled child. She liked Tehran, despite the pollution, religion, corruption, madness, and anger. Despite these things or because of them? She usually wondered. It felt like being inside a piece of postmodern art. She loved Tehran because that was where her father had died and where her mother lived. She would become successful in Tehran, like her mother. She did not mind the compulsory *hejab*, unlike many of her friends who constantly complained about it. She found it funny, ironic, to wear a *hejab*, to cover your sins, to exchange numbers with cologne-scented boys while being undercover. It was like being a spy. It was a game, and she knew she would win. Because she was clever, like her dead father and her lively mother.

*

5

When she reached the Ministry of Culture and Islamic Guidance, her body started trembling. It was not just the enormousness of the building that was unnerving: there was something inexplicably intimidating about it. It was situated inside an organised garden, with security guards looking like soldiers. The building itself was an enormous brown cube.

Two guards pounced in front of her. 'Ma'am, where are you going?'

'I have an appointment. At nine.' Sogol whispered, looking at the grey ground.

'With whom? And why?

'Regarding my poetry book, with Mr Mohammadi.'

'Okay, go.' They let her pass through the bars into the glossy building. All the newly published books were on display; she stood and looked at them. *The life of Imam Ali*, *The Holy Wars of the Prophet Muhammad*, *The Different Interpretations of Baghareh Sura*, *Hazrat-e Fatemeh and Her Holy Life*. Sogol was stunned. Where was all the poetry? All the books she always purchased from the bookshops? Sohrab Sepehri, Forough Farrokhzad, Ahmad Shamloo, translations of Plath, Lorca, and Neruda. There was no trace of them, they obviously did not belong in the display of the Ministry of Culture and Islamic Guidance. She laughed at her own naiveté. She relished the hypocrisy in a strange way, just as she was revelling in wearing a black chador. It was all a game, and unlike her friends, she knew how to play.

She took the lift to the fourth floor to Mr Mohammadi's office. Sogol was ready to express to a hideous, bearded man how she was an Islam–loving poet. That she was chaste.

And she was pure. She found the office and saw there were a few other people in the sunny room behind their desks: a few men and one woman. The woman was also wrapped in a black chador – Sogol felt vaguely victorious, terrified, and confident.

'*Salam,*' she smiled at the unfriendly woman. 'I am looking for Mr Mohammadi,' Sogol was careful not even to look at the men, that was how chaste she was acting. Not even one look at the *namahram*. Before the woman opened her mouth, one of the men emerged in front of her, unsmiling.

'That's me.'

Sogol was speechless. Mr Mohammadi looked the opposite of what she had in mind. To start with, he was clean-shaven. Milky skin, no trace of a stain, acne or beard on his smooth face. His eyes were light blue, matching his shirt, his brown eyelashes draping his eyes. Sogol looked down. She could stare at the physical beauty of Mr Mohammadi for hours if she let herself, but that was the wrong place and time, and he was the wrong person. She looked down at his shoes, shiny black, like wet nights after snow.

'I . . .'

'What do you want, ma'am?' Mr Mohammadi was 'licking her with his eyes', as her friends would've said.

'Mr Afshar told me to come here, to see whether or not my book has been granted permission for publication.'

'What is your book called?'

'*Earthquake in Ruins.*'

'Oh yes, let me see,' Mr Mohammadi sat behind his computer and began scrolling up and down for about fifteen minutes, then he murmured, 'It's number 18653279.'

'Thanks!' Sogol said.

'We don't know yet,' Mr Mohammadi shot her another blue glance. 'It is still being processed.'

Sogol wanted to scream. It was more than a year now. She was twenty-two when her mother had found her a publisher who would publish the poems. She fought hard not to say anything and to be polite. 'All right, thank you very much.'

'Goodbye.' Mr Mohammadi didn't even look at her.

On her way out, Sogol was holding onto her chador so that it wouldn't fall. She hated the fact that she felt like sobbing. She walked quickly, unable to wait to leave that monstrous building, to get rid of the suffocating chador, and to return to the safety of home.

She was walking out of the garden of the Ministry of Guidance into the empty alley when Mr Mohammadi pounced in front of her. Sogol thought, *what a strange coincidence*, until Mr Mohammadi told her, 'Look, I didn't want to say it in front of my colleagues, but your book has been deemed immoral. Therefore, it has been refused permission.'

Sogol opened her mouth without uttering a word, then closed it. Mr Mohammadi had more to say to her, 'But I really want to help you'.

Sogol avoided his eyes, not because she wanted to look chaste, but because she realised she could not tolerate his heavy glances at her lips. 'I will call you on Friday to tell you how to fix the problems if you want.'

'That is terribly kind of you. Thank you, I will fix everything you say is problematic.'

'You're not married, are you? Would it be okay if I called?' Mr Mohammadi said, stepping closer to Sogol.

'I'm not married,' Sogol muttered.

Mr Mohammadi took out his Nokia mobile, 'What is your number then?'

Sogol recited her mobile number, wanting to escape. Mr Mohammadi repeated the number to her before saving it, slowly stepping closer.

Sogol could not move. A car passed by. To Sogol's relief, Mr Mohammadi stepped back and said, 'I'll call you to discuss this. Bye for now.' And turned towards the direction of the Ministry.

Sogol ran all the way back to the crowded *taksi* station.

Kurt Cobain was screaming in her ears and she was staring at the traffic in order to withhold her tears. She loathed them. She detested her weakness. She wished she could be like her mother, if a man had talked to her mother like that, her mother would've strangled him. Her mother wouldn't have been a pushover like her, ready to be abused by a beautiful hypocrite in order to get her books published. Her mother was genuine. Sogol was fake, like her chador, her affectation of innocence and chastity, fake like her poetry. She did not deserve to get published. She was shedding tears, and noticed she couldn't even hear Kurt Cobain, because the taxi driver was screaming at someone in the traffic, calling another driver a 'whore's son', *'madar jendeh'*. Sogol took off her chador and headphones, pushing them into her black bag, and realised her phone was ringing. It was a new number. Mr Mohammadi's lustful tone of voice filled her ears like poison, 'Are you free on Friday?'

'Yes! I can even come to your office tomorrow,' Sogol said, trembling.

'Oh, but the Ministry is closed on Fridays! We have to meet someplace else!' Mr Mohammadi murmured, 'How about my flat?'

Sogol did not know how to respond. She felt like holding her phone to the sweary mouth of the *taksi* driver.

'Where do you live?' Sogol asked, not wanting to miss out on this ugly opportunity.

'East Tehran.'

Sogol had a vivid premonition of herself in Mr Mohammadi's claustrophobic flat in polluted East Tehran, stripped and shivering, Mr Mohammadi forcing her to kneel on his carpetless floor. Sogol whispered to her phone, 'Can I call you back?' and hung up, pushing against the other passengers sitting beside her. The taxi stopped near her house, opposite Mr Bahman's corner shop. Sogol paid the driver and got out of the car.

Their house was strangely quiet because her mother was out with her friends. Sogol slept for five hours, dreaming of fire, of Mr Mohammadi running after her in empty alleys with his repulsive beauty, and instead of a penis, he had a pen hanging out between his skinny white thighs. and Sogol was running, not wanting to be skewered by that cheap Bic biro. She kept running until she was woken by the sound of her mother, talking on the phone, laughing, and Sogol left her sweaty bed, finding it hard to breathe, galloping to her mother. Her mother hung up, looking worried, 'What is wrong, my darling?'

Sogol told her everything, everything about Mr Mohammadi, about his long lashes, his devouring blue eyes, his 'offer of help', the published books on the display of the Ministry, the garden, the taxi driver using swear words when Mr Mohammadi called – she recounted this to make the whole episode sound funny, but her mother was furious. Her mother wasn't laughing, she was shaking with fury. 'How dare he?' her mother exclaimed, 'Call him, tell him what he is doing is illegal, tell him he has no right to abuse his power, tell him to fuck himself, call him. Now!'

'Calm down, *maman*.'

'Get me some water,' her mother said.

Sogol brought out the cold bottle of water from the fridge. She poured two glasses, giving one to her mother, slurping the other herself. 'Don't even call him. Just completely ignore him. Let him die, filthy piece of shit!'

Sogol laughed. She went to her room, she called him from her mobile, 'I consulted with my mother. She says this is supposed to be a formal process. This is not how it should be.' After a few seconds of stony silence his informal, aggressively flirtatious tone changed into a formal one. 'Okay, ma'am. Whatever suits you. *Ensha'allah* the answer will be positive.' As if this were a pregnancy test. He hung up without saying goodbye. Sogol knew her book would not be published. But she was not sad.

Then the sound of the kettle filled her room; this was the music she loved the most; her mother was making tea.

An Evening of Martyrdom

They were playing cards, and Mina was losing. Attempting to console herself, she thought, *this isn't about losing or winning, only playing.*

She then tried to distract herself, concentrating more on the music and less on her losing and bad luck. But the music was no good – something loud and happy – which only intensified her ennui.

She downed her glass of whisky and coke, thinking the whisky was definitely fake, because it tasted like acetone, but still better than nothing. Tonight was the night of mourning for Imam Hossein, for whom the whole nation was supposed to wear black, weeping over his historic martyrdom in mosques reeking of rotten socks. So, drinking acetone-tasting whisky and losing at cards while listening to pop music was perhaps something to feel grateful about and to thank God for – except that she did not believe in God, so she carried on being annoyed and bored.

Mina looked up from her cards to glance at her *Hokm* teammate, a woman she'd just met. The woman caught Mina's attention and looked back at her with worried eyes which seemed to her as though they'd been drawn by Modigliani: they were mysterious, slanted. Mina was wondering how much her masterfully-drawn eyeliner played a role in creating this effect. She then noticed that the woman's face was also as long as the kind of face that Modigliani would paint. She desired to draw the woman, to see her naked. Her skin, Mina concluded, was the smoothest.

Upon her arrival, Mina had decided the boy sitting beside her had the most aesthetically pleasing features in the group, but he had stubble that Mina knew would feel anything but smooth. She also noticed that his hands were large and very hairy.

Sipping her whisky, Mina carried on losing, not caring about the game anymore. Suddenly, the music changed to one of her favourite songs – Not Gonna Get Us by t.A.T.u – so she nodded her head and looked at the woman, smiling, flashing her set of straight teeth. The woman smiled back and narrowed her eyes.

There were around fifteen people, eight of whom were playing cards and the rest were talking and smoking weed. Mina could hear their stoned laughter. For a moment, she felt insecure and scared, remembering Omid's neighbours preparing their place for a fine night of mourning. She had seen the black flags hanging from their windows and door – like corpses of infants. She had also seen something else that had moved her, even though she was reluctant to admit it.

Just as she was ringing Omid's doorbell, she saw two figures in black chador, standing on the doorstep of Omid's neighbour. They looked at her just as she was looking at them, one of them, an elderly woman, horribly solemn and the other, a teenage girl, probably a bit younger than Mina.

Their eyes met; Mina immediately wanted to antagonise her and the likes of her and everything she stood for, but she couldn't as the girl had the most innocent eyes she'd ever seen. And as her hair and body were fully covered with the long chador, Mina could only see her small face with light brown eyes and pale skin. The contrast of her complexion and her chador moved her like a Frida Kahlo's painting, it was so gloomy. The fact that she did not seem hostile at all disturbed Mina even more. For one insane moment, she was going to ask her to join the party; to dance and flirt and drink with them, to celebrate the enthralling nothingness of life with her and her friends, to embrace her youth and beauty, instead of praying in Arabic and forcing herself to weep for a man who had died centuries ago in some war that did not matter anymore.

Mina could not decipher what was in the girl's eyes. It was nothing like hostility or arrogance, more like innocence and confusion.

'What are you staring at?' the older woman barked.

'Nothing.' The girl said under her breath, averting her eyes from Mina and turning her back on her.

'Ah! Her terrible *hejab*?'

What struck Mina was that the woman didn't even lower her voice while trashing her. 'People like her end up in hell! And on such a sacred night . . . they can't even behave themselves for one night!'

'I know.' The girl mumbled.

Mina wanted to trash the woman back, to defend her beliefs, to discuss hell and heaven on earth with her, and eventually rescue the girl, but they disappeared into the neighbours' enormous house.

This was two hours ago and now Mina was losing the game like she lost the girl.

Then she remembered how her father had warned her to be extremely cautious. Mina knew her father would've asked her to stay home had he been a strict parent. She looked at her watch, it was half past nine; too early to get bored or annoyed or to miss her father's face.

Omid brought some fresh cookies from the kitchen with a new bottle of whisky. Mina took one cookie, and thanked him. She looked at the guests, their physicality and style, weighing up which one would be the most interesting to draw. The woman with Modigliani eyes in the fiery red dress was still at the top of her list. She was now lying on the floor, smoking a cigarette. Mina noticed the butt of her cigarette had a golden stain: the residue of her golden lips. She wished she had been a smoker, so she could ask for a cigarette or a lighter. Nevertheless, she sauntered over to her, unsure of how to start a conversation.

The woman sat up and gave Mina a shiny smile. Mina wondered if her golden lip gloss tasted sweet and chemical, or salty and sticky.

'No luck tonight, right?' the woman said, gracing Mina with her gilded smile.

They sat side by side on the carpeted floor.

'Right,' Mina replied, wondering what else she should say to maintain the conversation, when Omid interrupted them like a saviour.

'I'm such an idiot! My god. I should've introduced you to each other much sooner.'

'Why?' the woman asked, raising an eyebrow. Mina found this remark a little blunt, but laughed anyway.

'Well, it's so interesting. Mina studies art . . . painting . . . and you study architecture. And, well, you're both gorgeous!' Omid chuckled.

'Oh, that is an interesting way of reasoning.' She said, maintaining eye contact with Mina the whole time. She stretched out her dainty hand. 'I'm Hasti. Delighted to meet you.'

'Told you so, a perfect match!' Omid giggled, as a tall boy with green hair dragged him away to dance with him.

Mina realised she was still holding Hasti's cool hand. She dropped it awkwardly and asked her which university she was studying at, and if she was also from Shiraz.

'I'm also from Shiraz. But I've been living in Vienna for the past few years,' Hasti informed her. 'Now I'm here for a visit.'

'So, how are you finding Vienna?'

'Nice, can't really complain; although I miss Shiraz so much.'

'Why? I'm sure it's way better than here!'

'Yes, that's what you're supposed to say, I guess,' Hasti said, staring into space. 'I find most Austrians a bit like robots, even the good ones. The bad ones are just old-fashioned fascists.'

Mina was uncertain what Hasti was ranting about. Was she just being a bored, rich bitch? Wasn't Austria supposed to be the beating heart of the arts? 'I heard they are very disciplined?' Mina said.

'Good for them,' Hasti puffed her cigarette. 'But I like a bit of chaos, passion – oh, and dark eyes!' She gazed into Mina's eyes through the smoke and Mina felt weak, realising she was unable to disagree with her.

*

It was about eleven when they resumed playing cards. This time, Mina felt fortunate and energetic. Omid refilled their glasses with whisky, and emptied the ashtray cluttered with Hasti's golden cigarette butts. Mina and Hasti won a round. Mina almost shouted with joy, and Hasti beamed.

Mina and Hasti won the second round with a bit of cheating as well, which excited Mina even more. Hasti sneakily peeked at the other players' cards, and Mina signalled to her which one to play first. Everybody else seemed too intoxicated to understand or even care about what was going on. Omid lay on the carpet, his head resting on Mina's lap. She was now trembling with exhilaration, the whisky not working on her. She was waiting to win the entire set, so she could smoke weed with Hasti, and probably talk to her about Zaha Hadid or music flirtatiously, or about how Austria sucks and Iran rocks, therefore Hasti should stay in Iran, or maybe just look at her wordlessly, absorbing her beauty.

The album finished, and there was no more loud music; the living room was filled with the vague sound of the neighbours mourning Imam Hossein. Nobody said anything; the people who were talking and laughing on the other side of the room suddenly went silent.

The voice of the mullah singing in a miserable tone about the martyrdom of Imam Hossein filled the room. *And his little son . . . they didn't let him have any water . . . oh God, oh God, oh God . . . he was only three . . . Oh God, oh God, oh God . . .'* followed by the sound of the weeping of the people in the neighbourhood.

Mina wondered if the girl was weeping along with the crowd or not. Was she bored to tears or moved by those melodramatic fables sold to her as historical facts? Mina wondered if they were purely fabricated, or if there was a grain of truth in them. But she was too tired to question her own beliefs, too respectful towards life to appreciate something hellish. She felt agitated, dizzy and nauseated; as thirsty as Imam Hossein's son. Fearing the fake whisky might blind or poison her, she presumed if God wasn't dead after all, he would definitely punish her, would definitely put her in hell, like that woman had said. She thought about how her poor father would feel about her death or disease due to bad whisky. After all, hadn't he had enough?

Finally one of the guests addressed Omid: 'Honey, are you sure this is okay? I'm thinking maybe this wasn't the right night to party.'

'Don't be silly,' Omid laughed. 'In fact, this is the *best* time for a little partying, as my parents are on a trip because of this national holiday for the martyrdom of our beloved Hossein, and I have the *whole* house to myself!' He wasn't lying on the floor anymore and busied himself with the stereo.

'Okay then. But let's keep it quiet,' another guest suggested.

'Guys! No need to be scared,' a woman with dyed blonde hair roared from the other side of the living room.

Mina looked at her from afar, and felt grateful that Hasti had kept her hair dark and natural, unlike most women Mina had met. No wonder she never felt anything for them, never felt like drawing them or touching them. Hasti's olive skin was glowing, her cheekbones highlighted with golden powder. Mina felt even more enchanted by her looks.

For a moment Mina forgot about the neighbours and the girl. Hasti asked Omid to play some 50 Cent, and Mina caught Hasti looking at her, at her neck and breasts, and she felt fortunate for feeling free and looking great, for having the same dark hair and complexion as Hasti's, for not having coarse stubble like most of the boys at the party. And thought how she abhorred the fads in Shiraz imported from Hollywood. How grotesque and unnatural they made people look; and how ever-lasting they seemed: the thickly-drawn or overly-plucked eye brows, the dyed hair, the fake-tanned skin, the pig noses – all looking the same thanks to plastic surgery. Then she forgot about criticising the fashion trends of her city, as she realised Hasti was mouthing the words to In Da Club, while looking at Mina and shaking her head, half-closing her eyes and looking completely carried away by the music. Mina wished she could understand what 50 Cent was saying, but English was always her worst subject at school.

Mina sipped her whisky, her eyes all over Hasti, until she felt Hasti's red dress was attacking her – like red coming out of a Mondrian composition, cruelly conquering the viewer, leaving her incapable of looking away, of escape.

Nobody was playing cards anymore: Omid was dancing with a few other boys, and the rest of the players were lying on the carpet, either high or drunk, laughing and greedily eating cookies, salad, nuts, and Omid's delectable *dolmehs*. Mina and Hasti were the only ones still holding onto their cards, staring at each other.

Finally, Hasti spilled her cards on the carpeted floor, letting them melt into the flowers of the intensely beautiful Persian carpet. As a result of smoking, drinking and nibbling, Hasti's lip gloss had come off and Mina found her unpainted lips with their natural, meaty colour even more appealing. She was already sniffing the scent of her neck when Hasti grabbed her right hand and murmured, 'Let's go.' Mina did not know where, but followed her nevertheless.

Hasti and Mina were walking in a narrow corridor with orange wallpaper, hand in hand, Hasti a few steps ahead, leading Mina. Mina's nostrils were on Hasti's nape, sniffing its strange scent, which Mina concluded smelt like her dead mother: a mixture of cigarette smoke and spicy cologne, resulting in a scent of burnt trees, which she relished. She sensed her next painting would be a forest on fire. She knew Hasti was taking her to Omid's bedroom, at the end of the long corridor. Suddenly she felt in love with the existence of this corridor, which connected Omid's living room to his bedroom, separating her and Hasti from the rest of the party. It was indeed the best thing that could exist in a house, and probably in the world.

However, the time was not the best time; Mina noticed the black clock with golden numbers hanging on the wall of the corridor showing a quarter past one. She thought of her father, and heard the sound of the wailing of Omid's neighbours at a higher volume than when they were in the living room. It was probably because there was no music in the corridor. And yet, Hasti's movements and presence were the most powerful piece of music.

'How old are you, by the way?' Mina asked Hasti.

'Twenty-seven. Why?' Hasti replied, her cold hand pressing on Mina's bare arm.

'Just curious. I'm turning twenty in a week. You should come to my birthday party. Omid's also coming.' She felt frivolous for having said all this in her drunken voice. Hasti didn't say anything, just pushed her into Omid's bedroom: the promised land.

The room was dark and quiet. Mina noticed the neighbours had finally stopped wailing, but for a moment she wished they had not stopped, as the silence was even more suffocating.

She opened the curtains and the light of the night poured into the dark room; the moon was full, and Mina felt insecure. Hasti pushed her onto the bed. Mina pushed her back.

'I need to tell you something,' murmured Mina.

'What? You want to know my surname?' Hasti let out a nervous laugh at her own joke, which Mina found too crude, almost cruel.

'No.' Mina retorted while Hasti was undressing. The red dress was gone in a moment, thrown to the floor.

Mina found herself touching Hasti's breasts with the tip of her trembling fingers. Hasti grabbed her hand and stopped her. 'What? You're not on your period, are you?'

'No.'

'Thank God!'

'But . . .' Mina paused, and gazed into Hasti's eyes in the dark. Hasti put her arms around her with force.

'But what? You're killing me.'

'This is my first time.' Mina said, feeling hot with embarrassment, inebriation and desire.

'You mean you're a virgin?'

'Yes,' Mina murmured, kissing her lips tenderly. Hasti's mouth tasted like a pack of cigarettes.

'Oh,' Hasti sighed. 'Don't worry. That turns me on.' and took off Mina's black top under which her breasts were waiting to be released from the tyranny of her bra.

Mina was pleased that Hasti was 'turned on' by her confession and not taken aback. Hasti's cold fingers started running all over her body. Mina closed her eyes and let herself tremble on Omid's single bed.

When Hasti's sharp teeth reached her nipples, nothing was dark anymore, but orange and gold. Mina opened her eyes and realised Hasti's beauty, her sharp cheekbones, were enhanced by the half-dark room.

'My god ... you are so gorgeous it's agonising.' Mina found herself saying and regretting it, fearing Hasti might find this remark too old-fashioned, over the top, or desperate. But Hasti smiled and said, 'So are you!'

For a moment, Mina felt as though she was looking in the mirror while masturbating, so she grabbed Hasti's long neck and sniffed it some more, trying to block out the thought of her dead mother smelling exactly the same. She then plunged her teeth in her neck and wanted to stay there forever.

'Aw!' Hasti complained. 'You like it rough?'

Mina did not reply; for some reason she could not talk. She was breathing heavily and the only thing she cared about was her heavenly wetness and Hasti's wet mouth. Hasti's fingers were inside her and Mina was writhing on the dark bed trying her best not to scream.

The door opened, and she felt blinded by the orange corridor and the figure of someone she didn't recognise in her inebriation, orgasm and the dark.

'The neighbours have called the police.' The figure said, her voice quiet and quivering.

Mina suddenly remembered she was one of the guests playing cards with them earlier. The dizziness of her pleasure turned into a sudden pang of pain, and she tried to push Hasti away, but Hasti bit her right ear and whispered, 'Sorry, I can't stop. You're too hot.' She used the actual English word 'hot', pronouncing it like 'haat' which would both annoy and please Mina under different circumstances, but now only angered and frightened her more. She felt Hasti's breath was the only hot thing, as it was piercing her skin, so she yelled, 'Get off me!' and took Hasti's slender shoulders in her nails and this time pushed her away with more force.

Mina picked some other guest's scarf and *manteau* from Omid's closet and covered her shaking, naked body. For a moment it occurred to Mina that Hasti was insane for not being as scared as her, and at this thought she felt even more afraid.

Hasti was laughing bitterly at her, still lying naked on Omid's bed. 'Don't worry, little girl. We'll give some cash to those bastards and they won't harm us.'

Mina felt deaf and blind, and incandescent. All the stories and news she'd heard about people being lashed, imprisoned, and even executed for alcohol and homosexual sex started revolving in her head like a poisonous tornado. She was not sure what her punishment would be, but she knew it would be massive. She knew she was a criminal and her whole existence a terrible crime.

'Come on, darling!' Hasti was not giving up. 'I haven't had my orgasm yet.' And chuckled, sitting up on the bed. 'You're a selfish little girl, aren't you?'

Mina wanted to respond by telling Hasti that this was not Vienna and it was dangerous, but she could not. Hasti's radiant figure on the bed already looked like a beautiful memory from the past. It dawned on Mina that the future was going to be even darker than Omid's room. She opened the door to the sordid corridor, and felt like exploding in the middle of the living room; the image of her limbs scattered across the threads of the fine Persian carpet in front of all those guests sickened her, and she vomited, awaiting her arrest.

It was then that she noticed there was no one else in the living room. All the lights were on, they were probably hiding somewhere, she thought miserably as she ran towards the door, not even having wiped the translucent vomit from her mouth, its sourness burning her throat.

Her right foot hit a line of glasses on the floor and she fell down, feeling the wetness of the liquor between her toes, and shortly afterwards an unbearable pain in her right calf. She sat in the middle of the lonely living room and wept, waiting for the morality police to come and take her. She imagined her father's shock after being informed at five in the morning about the arrest of her homosexual daughter at a sinful party on such a sacred night. She wept like Omid's neighbours, and was enraged and helpless, knowing with the current condition of her right foot, she couldn't escape from the police, and that this was the definition of misery.

Suddenly it occurred to her that she was more miserable than that girl in the chador: at least she wouldn't be arrested, she was safe and sound like 'a pearl in its shell' – as written on the billboards of the city – fitting in well, accepted and accepting of her condition. Mina concluded she needed to pity herself instead of that girl. She felt worse than the time she was informed about the accident that led to her mother's death – back when she was fourteen, sexless, and sober.

Mina was wondering if the police would take her to the doctor first, for her foot, or if they wouldn't believe her and would just push her in the direction of wherever the hell they were taking her. Her whole body was shaking from this thought, when the dyed-blonde woman with the fake tan and the fake lashes appeared in the living room and embraced her. 'Ah, don't worry. They fucked off. Omid bribed them.' And she laughed at Mina's wet eyes.

Mina could not even pretend to laugh. For some reason, this piece of good news did not make her happy, only empty. The pain in her foot was worsening by the second. She bit her bottom lip so she wouldn't cry.

Omid and some of the other guests came back in the living room, speaking in subdued but excited tones, making odd laughing noises. Omid recounted how he bribed the police in the tone of a sarcastic war hero, even though there was still the trace of a tremor in his voice.

The green-haired boy was drinking from the bottle of whisky, laughing madly at Omid's words, his lean body shaking.

When Mina turned, she saw that Hasti was sitting on the sofa, in her red dress again, her longish hair dishevelled. Her eyeliner was smudged, making her eyes look round rather than slanted, inhaling and exhaling her perpetual cigarette, looking attentively at Omid, with the trace of a surreptitious smile on her face.

Mina dried her face, trying her best to ignore her pain. But when she looked around, she concluded that they were just a bunch of strangers; she sensed she didn't know any of the people here – especially herself.

Caspian

Mojgan couldn't concentrate on her *namaz*. 'Ashhadu alla ilaha illallah . . .' *How many pairs of knickers should I take with me for three days?* 'Assalamu alaikum wa rahmatullahi wa barakatuh.'

She kissed the clay *mohr,* took off her floral chador and folded her embroidered *janamaz.*

Tonight, she was too excited to read the Quran. Also, she needed to pack and it was already nine.

Her parents were asleep, but she knew Mohammad was awake, probably staring at his computer screen, his long lashes motionless. Mojgan and her mother and aunts always laughed at God's sense of humour for granting her brother such affluent lashes while giving her almost none. Her mother bought tubes of mascara to fix this 'issue', but Mojgan had an allergic reaction to even the most expensive ones. Besides, she secretly hated makeup. She wanted to look as innocent as possible. Like the mental image she had of Hazrat-e Fatemeh. Except she didn't want to die yet, even though Mojgan was almost the same age at which Hazrat-e Fatemeh had become a martyr: eighteen. Mojgan wanted to go to university and become a physician.

At eleven o'clock, she knocked on Mohammad's door.

'Come in,' he whispered. Mojgan knew he'd close all the web pages and turn off that strange music before letting anyone in.

Mojgan sat on Mohammad's messy bed. It had a nice smell: Adidas cologne and the natural scent of his skin, which she'd loved since they were little.

'Why aren't you asleep yet?' Mohammad swung on his chair to face her, smiling. 'We're leaving early in the morning. Armin will pick us up at eight.'

'You can't wake up at eight,' Mojgan said, giggling.

'I'll have to – it's Armin's orders! And since he's driving and wants to avoid the traffic, we have to obey him . . . But we can sleep in the car.'

'What's his car?' Mojgan asked.

'Maxima. White.'

'So, they're rich?'

'I think so . . . His mother is a dentist.'

'That's so cool! Do you remember that time he came over here and Mum burnt the rice? So, we had to serve stew with bread . . .' Mojgan still recalled the burnt food, the stench of shame.

'How can I forget?' Mohammad chuckled. 'Are you all packed?'

'Yes! Are you sure you still want me to come? I feel kind of extra . . . Armin is your friend and there's no other girls . . . Isn't that a bit weird?'

'We'd love you to come! You need to see the Caspian sea. The sensation of floating on it is perfect.'

'Isn't it polluted, though?'

'Not as polluted as Tehran's air. Also, Armin's villa is in a nice area: Mahmood Abad. It's stunning . . . You have to come out of your shell and see the rest of your country – I want you to see new things. Mum and Dad haven't shown us much . . .'

Mojgan rejoiced in the memory of Mohammad arguing with her parents about letting her travel to the north. She never imagined they would agree. But Mohammad had won the argument by parading passionate logic.

'She needs to see the world. You're raising her like cave people!'

Her parents bitterly consented, under the condition that they would tell no one in the extended family. It had to remain their family secret. For good.

Mojgan knew Mohammad thought their parents were 'narrow-minded' and he worried about her. She also noticed Mohammad had stopped praying since he'd been accepted at the university. It pained her to think her brother might have become an apostate, but she dreaded even discussing it with him. She caught herself staring at her brother's smooth face. She knew how soft his skin was, like their mother's and unlike hers. And now it was glowing like the moon on its fourteenth night.

Mohammad caught her staring at him and smiled. 'You seem extremely excited about tomorrow!'

Mojgan blushed for a reason she couldn't fathom. 'I am! Also, slightly anxious . . . It's my first trip without Mum and Dad – well, apart from a few tedious school trips.'

'Travelling without authority is indeed sweet!' Mohammad said.

Mojgan wasn't sure what he meant, but she didn't ask for fear of sounding uneducated. Mohammad was becoming cleverer by the day. She was terrified of becoming distant from him. One day, she would find the courage to ask him about his new beliefs. And yet she wasn't sure how to handle his answer – which she already knew. She'd overheard her mother complaining to one of their aunts. 'He's just changed . . . I don't feel we can handle him anymore . . . He's become a new person since he met this glitzy boy Armin . . . Thank God, at least he's still on good terms with his sister, but he can't stand us . . . I've noticed he doesn't even pray any more, and when I questioned him, he yelled at me that he's sick of us and we shouldn't meddle in his private life. He's learned these vicious words from that sordid Armin.' And then her mother had burst out crying.

Mojgan asked her mother about it a few months ago. But her mother urged her to mind her own studies, so she too would get accepted by a good university, as her brother had.

Mojgan prayed and studied. Studied and prayed. Studied in the morning and prayed at night. She spent hours each day preparing herself for the university entrance exam in the summer. All the eighteen-year-olds from all over the country would participate in the exam. People spent their lives in preparation for it. Mohammad had turned out to be successful, as usual. He was accepted to study French Literature at Shahid Beheshti university. But still their parents had looked down on his choice of subject, even though he was already making money by tutoring French.

'What a strange major for a man!' their father declared when Mohammad gave them the good news.

'At least it's Shahid Beheshti, so we don't need to pay

for those expensive *azad* universities with no prestige,' her mother consoled herself.

Mohammad was too ecstatic to argue that day. He'd bought Mojgan a golden tube of sunscreen.

'I should be the one giving you a present!' Mojgan had happily objected.

Mohammad responded by embracing her tightly and kissing her forehead.

Mojgan was aware Mohammad's victories were also partly hers. Every night she prayed for him before falling asleep. Lying in bed under her floral duvet, she whispered: 'Dear God, I love you. But I also love my family. I want them to be always healthy. And please let me die before Mohammad will. Make me and Mohammad get accepted in *sarasari* universities, so our poor parents won't need to pay those illiterate *azad* universities. Dear God, help me become a doctor and save your creatures' lives.'

This had been the typical template of her nightly prayer for the last five years. It never bored her. And she always felt God was on her side.

In the morning, she was awoken by Mohammad and realised she'd shamefully fallen asleep on his bed. 'Where did you sleep?' she asked, her eyes wide.

'On your bed,' Mohammad said, giggling. 'Get up!'

Mojgan brushed her teeth in thirty seconds and put on a loose cotton *manteau* and a green headscarf.

Their father had left earlier for work; their mother was in the kitchen as usual, pouring tea, and staring at them anxiously.

'What if you get arrested on the road?' her mother finally

mumbled to Mohammad, who was hastily buttering a piece of *taftoon* bread.

'Why would they arrest us? We're related! Brother and sister!'

'Yes, but you are young, and Arman and Mojgan are *namahram*.'

Her mother would always intentionally call Armin 'Arman' to piss off Mohammad. And it did work. Every single time.

'Oh stop! Even *they* are not as *ommol* as you are!' Mohammad hissed.

'I'm just worried,' their mother hissed back. And Mojgan felt like choking on her *sangak* bread and feta cheese.

'Shall we go? Isn't Armin waiting?' Mojgan murmured.

Mohammad stood. 'Yes!'

Their mother also stood up. 'Hold on, I need to pass you under the Quran.'

Mojgan liked the idea; she couldn't wait to kiss the Quran while walking under it. It was her favourite tradition; it made her feel incredibly safe.

'Oh, for God's sake,' Mohammad said. 'Let's go.' He grabbed Mojgan's right hand. She couldn't help but feel exhilarated.

Nevertheless, their mother ran to bring a Quran. Mohammad ran out of the door and Mojgan kissed the Holy Book and walked under it as her mother held it above her head.

Then she held her mother for a second. 'Don't worry, we'll be safe. And I'll give you a call as soon as we get there.'

Armin was waiting in his car, a victorious ship outside their petty house. He was wearing sunglasses even though the weather was cloudy.

Mohammad sat beside him in the front and Mojgan sat on the back seat. She almost liked Armin when he opened the door for her, finding the gesture unexpectedly gentlemanly.

'Are we ready?' Armin asked, his voice energetic.

'Yeah!' Mohammad's mood had completely changed.

Unlike Mohammad, Armin was growing a bit of stubble. Mojgan decided it suited him, then blushed at the idea. She didn't want to end up like some of her classmates, drowning in the perilous sea of boys, unable to concentrate on their studies. She didn't want a boyfriend or a husband. She wanted a hospital filled with ill people whom she could cure. She also wanted to earn money and buy her parents a bigger house, a better life. She craved to travel to Mecca to visit the House of God with her family. But Mohammad had already declared that he'd rather travel to France, where he understood 'la langue', rather than to Saudi Arabia. Perhaps he'd change his mind by then; he'd lose interest in Armin and his Ray-Ban sunglasses and deep voice and charming manners and would resume appreciating God and Mecca.

Mojgan realised Armin and Mohammad weren't in the same university. She found it odd, as she'd always assumed they were classmates and that was how they met. Armin was quietly asking Mohammad about his university, and Mohammad Armin about his.

Mojgan deciphered that the music in Armin's ship was the same as the music she could hear from Mohammad's room when she pushed her ears against his wall. A mellow, depressing tune with a person – she wasn't sure of their gender – moaning in English. Mojgan couldn't get all of the song, only a few words and phrases she'd learned at school. She was worried about not doing well in English in the entrance exam. Listening carefully to the song, she was pleased to distinguish words such as 'death', 'distance' (a word she'd recently learned), 'love', and 'painless'. The song was relaxing and when she heard Mohammad murmuring, 'She fell asleep . . . isn't exactly a morning person,' she was praying they wouldn't get inspected by the road police. And then her slumber became even deeper as the music died away and Mohammad and Armin ceased their sibilant whispers.

In her sleep, Mojgan was in Mecca with Mohammad. Right in front of Ka'ba. Mojgan was crying tears of ecstasy while Mohammad said, 'What's the point of this empty black cube?' But Mojgan was too moved by the presence of God to be able to reply. God was inside her.

Her eyes blinked open and she caught a blurry glimpse of Armin's long hand resting a moment on her brother's jeaned thigh. She blinked again, and the hand was gone. She was certain she was seeing things, like the Mecca dream.

Why am I hallucinating so much? I need to study more, she concluded.

She looked out of the window at the serpentine maze of Chalous Road, partly tunnelled by bright green trees, and at times surrounded by the Alborz mountains. Mohammad was right, this was much more beautiful than Tehran. Tehran was gregariously grey, and this was gloriously green. Mojgan imagined she was in heaven and felt pleasantly nauseous.

Then Armin exclaimed, 'Good morning!'

Mojgan giggled. 'I wasn't asleep,'

Mohammad winced, 'Weren't you? Really?'

34

'Oh, I was!' Mojgan reassured him. 'I even had a dream.'

'Of what?' Armin asked. Mojgan found herself liking the interest he expressed.

'Just the sea,' she said, sensing she shouldn't talk to Armin about her love for God. 'I haven't been in the Caspian since I was five.'

Mohammad would be hurt; he would think she was like their mother: '*ommol*'.

'It hasn't changed much,' Armin said. 'You'll see. And you'll love it.'

At one o'clock they arrived in Mahmood Abad. Armin parked his Maxima outside a restaurant.

'This is my favourite eatery in *shomal*.'

The restaurant was crowded, nonetheless, they were given a corner table where Mojgan was pulverised under the weight of customers' glances. They were scrutinising her chaste *hejab*, looking like a good girl while being with two handsome boys. 'A total whore' – she could almost hear their verdict, like some of her classmates who loved using the word: '*jendeh*'.

'What do you fancy?' Armin handed the enormous menu to Mohammad, studying his face, and then looked away to stare at the greasy salt shaker.

'Fish, naturally!'

'I recommend the white fish with herbed rice and *kookoo sabzi*.'

'I don't want to get fat,' Mohammad said, laughing.

'You'll never get fat!' Armin glanced at him again. This time they both looked away, averting their eyes to Mojgan as though suddenly remembering her presence.

Mojgan wanted to sound like them. She felt like playing along. 'What's the best meal I can have in here, Armin?' It was the first time she'd addressed him by name and she wished she could stop blushing like a silly fourteen-year-old girl.

'If you like fish, get either the white fish or the trout.'

Mojgan wanted to get the same fish as Mohammad, but heard herself saying, 'I'll go for the trout.'

A waiter took their orders with a short stubby pencil. Mojgan wondered whether it felt uncomfortable in his massive hand. Armin smiled at him, and also ordered *zeytoon parvardeh* and garlic pickle, excitedly informing Mohammad and Mojgan that their olives were 'ace'.

The food smelled like the sea. Mojgan ate it all, despite the fact that it made her slightly sick.

When all their plates were empty, Armin asked for the bill.

Then Armin and Mohammad argued charmingly about who should pay.

'You're my guests,' Armin exclaimed while showering Mohammad with his convincing smile, his teeth even whiter than his skin.

'But you'll be cooking for us, won't you?' Mohammad protested. 'Look, I really want to pay this time. You can get dinner.'

'No way!' Armin was invincible. 'We won't have dinner, we'll feel full until tomorrow morning, believe me.'

'Then be responsible for our lunch tomorrow.'

'No, I brought you here,' Armin insisted. 'You can take me to a restaurant you like in Tehran. Take me to that new Lebanese restaurant you've been raving about.'

Mohammad finally allowed Armin to pay.

On the way to the car, Mojgan noticed Mohammad's slender body was closer to Armin's than to hers. Something burnt inside her.

When they were finally inside the vast villa, it was three o'clock. Armin appointed them each a room. Mojgan had been hoping she'd share with her brother like when they were children.

The room was cleaner than her own room in Tehran. There were pale blue sheets on the single bed, a bedside table with a lamp, and a full bookcase. She took off her *manteau* and took out a long-sleeved shirt from her backpack, wearing it with matching white pyjama trousers: comfy and chaste. She didn't touch her headscarf, a light material which didn't feel suffocating like some others. It felt right.

Mojgan scrutinised the bookshelves. There was no Quran. Instead, they were infested with Sadegh Hedayat's books. She disliked Hedayat, even though she'd never read him. He was a pre-revolutionary Islam-loathing existentialist who wrote depressing literature and ended up gassing himself in Paris or some other pretentious place. And yet he was never out of fashion. He was considered trendy and classy and this was what repelled Mojgan more than anything. She knew Mohammad loved him. He had praised *The Blind Owl* like every other unique youngster who studied art and literature.

Mojgan picked up *The Blind Owl,* lay on the comfortable bed and couldn't stop reading the sickly prose. Mohammad knocked on her door asking whether she'd go to the beach with them.

'I'm pleased you're reading him at last. But you can also read in our own sea-less city,' Mohammad commented. Mojgan noticed he looked as darkly beautiful as the ethereal object of desire of the insane narrator.

'I'm tired.'

'From what? Sleeping and eating?'

'The journey, the car, the road.'

'You're just a lazy little girl,' Mohammad told her teasingly, catching her eyes.

'I'll join you later. I know where the beach is.'

'It's very close. Just step out of the house and bang the door shut, and you'll probably see us in the sea, I'm glad there aren't many people; because it's spring they find the sea cold and sometimes stormy . . . but I say the spring sea is the best sea – especially with all those *ommol* tacky people out of the picture . . .'

Mojgan laughed.

Once Mohammad had left, she couldn't concentrate on the rest of the novel. She didn't want to. When she read it, she felt as depressed and hallucinatory as the substance-abusing narrator. And she remembered she hadn't done her noon *namaz*. As she went to the sparkling bathroom to *vozu*, the silence told her Mohammad and Armin were gone. She was alone in the villa.

Pouring water on her arms, feet and head, she caught a glimpse of her face in the bathroom mirror. For once she didn't avoid her dark eyes. She stared at her invisible lashes and sighed for Mohammad's long ones. Her face was fat, an ill-looking balloon, unlike Mohammad's and Armin's. They had slim faces and even, high cheekbones like the ethereal girl in *The Blind Owl*. They could melt the world with the sun in their eyes. Mojgan wondered why she had such small eyes. Aren't all Iranians supposed to have huge eyes? Perhaps she wasn't a true Persian like Mohammad, but was an adopted Afghan refugee. She wished her parents would tell her the truth. She leaned in to the mirror but felt an involuntary shudder; she scorned her childish fantasies, realising she was acting like some of her brainless classmates, who weren't really studying but were merely obsessing over the appearance of actors.

Mojgan sauntered back to her new room, took out her chador and *mohr* from her rucksack and did her noon and evening *namaz* in ten minutes, all the while imagining herself in the endless Caspian sea with Mohammad and Armin, floating, and jumping over the waves, living life to the fullest and yet being virtuous enough to go to heaven after her death in a hundred years or so. Pleasing God and people at the same time, but also pleasing herself. She could have it all. Why not?

It was eight and the sea was getting dark. 'The bright side is there are no *ommol* tacky people in the sea now.' Her brother's voice echoed in her brain. Did Mohammad find her 'tacky' and '*ommol*', with her chaste *hejab*, prayers, fat face and small eyes?

She saw Armin and Mohammad from afar.

She saw Armin in Mohammad's thin, yet powerful arms.

They were jumping and laughing in the wavy sea. There was no one else around. No *ommol* tacky people.

The air was humid. She stood, worrying about – she didn't even know exactly what. Mohammad's back was to her. They wouldn't even think about her. She was irrelevant and *ommol*. With her *hejab*, prayers, studies, Godly goals, chastity and lack of knowledge of music and French and Sadegh Hedayat.

Standing on the beach, in her tight headscarf, she couldn't even hear them, but she could see their laughter, their joy. Then she finally saw. She saw her brother biting Armin's neck while rising and falling with the waves, except that Mohammad didn't look like her brother any longer; he looked like a violent animal preying on male flesh. She saw Armin swiftly kissing her brother's parted lips. The kiss must taste salty and polluted like the Caspian sea.

She hadn't seen anything like this, even in the Hollywood movies her classmates convinced her to watch under the pretext of improving her English. There was always a bulky brunette man making love to a bony blonde woman. Never two men kissing; two men as beautiful and as dark as Armin and Mohammad.

She knew of it; she'd read about it in the Quran a few years ago. *Ghome Lut*. And she knew perfectly well what the verdict for them would be. God disliked homosexuals. And that was the only thing she knew.

Then she recalled a night, two years ago, when she had innocently asked Mohammad whether he would like to marry a girl from his university. He laughed so hard she felt embarrassed and perplexed. And then he said, 'I have no interest in girls.' How naive and blind she had been. He had informed her. He wanted her to know. But how cruel of him to want her to know something so dreadful and dangerous. How could Mohammad be so ruthless and so sinful? With his name, identical to the Prophet Muhammad's, and his face as gorgeous as the Prophet Joseph's, and his voice as divine as the Prophet David's. How could this all be so meaningless?

And if this was the case, if her divine brother was ... indeed ... *hamjensbaz* ... why did he bring her here? To show her how irrelevant and worthless her religious beliefs were? To spit his perverse perfection in her imperfect face? To prove to her how *ommol* she was and he did not give a fuck? Or perhaps to use her as a shield, a cover for his homosexual trip?

Mojgan craved to be in Tehran. In her tiny room, studying Arabic, English and biology for *konkoor*, praying to get accepted by a good university. She did not like *shomal*.

Then she wondered why God had ordered for her brother and Armin to be executed. Allah, the all-kind and merciful. *Rahman* and *Rahim*. The all-forgiving God. The one and only *khoda*.

Armin and Mohammad were not in each other's arms. They were just both in the sea. Their torsos bare and wet, their dark swimsuits as tight as her headscarf, emphasising their depraved genitals.

Mojgan was still staring at the blackness of the sea. She dreaded to agree with Sadegh Hedayat, to acknowledge the darkness of life. She wanted to have both God and her brother. She wanted to please Mohammad and the Prophet Muhammad.

Armin finally noticed her and beckoned her to join them.

Mojgan threw herself into the sea. She could have everything now. She could float in the darkest waters, while being a good servant to God and go to heaven in the afterlife.

Mohammad jumped on her and shouted. She shouted

back, but it was hardly a scream, just a whimper. Armin looked at them with his adoring eyes and swam away. Mohammad swam after him. They went back to the beach. Lying on their straw mat, on the sinful sand.

The water was lukewarm, up to her waist. The waves were playful. She wanted to forget, but couldn't. Armin and Mohammad were lying beside each other, not touching, but it was now blindingly obvious. She made the knot on her headscarf tighter, so the waves couldn't steal her *hejab*. She let herself float under the stars. She'd forgotten how purifying it felt to be in the sea – especially in a polluted one. Not wanting to get out of the Caspian sea, she kept floating in the dark.

When she realised she couldn't breathe, and the waves were too powerful, the knot on her throat too tight, and her trousers unbearably heavy, it was too late to try.

She could hear her brother's hysterical roars and caught a glimpse of him swimming towards her with Armin following like a shark, but the waves pushed them away and pulled her down. Maybe God wasn't on her side after all. Only then did she remember she'd forgotten to call her mother. But it didn't matter any longer.

Mojgan imagined Mohammad gliding towards her with his salty eyelashes and sinful mouth. And she did not see heaven, but saw herself and her brother as children watching *Lucky Luke* and Mohammad stating, 'I love Luke! He's so handsome!'

Then she felt Mohammad's determined fingers clutch her arms. Now her mother had every right to worry.

Spoilt

Z ahra is pouring tea from the floral tea pot and she tells me she is happy for me. I am happy for me too.

We are sitting in Zahra's neat kitchen, the scorching sun of Tehran attacking our eyes. Zahra hands me a *fenjan* of black tea, and smiles. 'So, tell me, are you ready?'

'Yes! I've been ready for this university all my life.' Even though I have not stepped foot in it yet, I am already romanticising it.

Zahra slurps her tea, muttering, 'good.'

We don't have much to talk about. I think I love her – I think of her as my best friend – not just my cool cousin, but I have promised my mother not to share any of my 'secrets' with Zahra. 'They are different from us. And she will tell everyone.'

'Have you thought about what you're going to do after you get your bachelor's?'

'Nope!' I confess.

'Would you like to teach or something? Because that's the only job you could ever have with such a useless major!' Zahra informs me.

I sip my tea and it burns my tongue. Zahra has taken off her tight headscarf, and her pile of black hair seems dishevelled. Then she suddenly asks me, 'do you think you'll find a boyfriend at university? For some reason the idea of you getting married makes me laugh.'

'It makes me laugh, too.' I'm almost rolling on the kitchen floor, fighting the urge to inform her that I already have a lover to whom I can't see myself getting married; I'm only eighteen. Zahra is twenty-one, and is going out with one of her suitors. I know they don't touch each other, they eat kebab, and talk about cinema. My mother and I have a bet that they will get married within three weeks.

I push some fresh cookies into my mouth in order not to talk. My mother is screaming in my head, 'don't be silly!'

Zahra's fancy smart phone beeps the beep of a text message. She looks down and blushes.

'Who is it?' I ask, trying to sound mischievous like when we were children.

'I'm not telling,' she chuckles and thinks she's teasing me. This is no teasing; I know who it is. My mother's already told me everything she's heard from our grandmother.

'I know about Mehdi,' I say, tired of keeping secrets.

'Oh my god, who told you?' she asks, offended.

'I don't know. Everyone knows everything in this family.'

'I know! It's so annoying!'

'Do you like him?' I ask her. I find myself worrying about her. How can she marry a guy she has never touched? What if he's sexually dysfunctional? What if he beats her?

'I do!' Zahra looks down, the way chaste female characters do in our national TV shows.

'Does he have a beard?' I don't know why I ask this question.

'He does! But I like it . . . I like men to be rugged,' Zahra declares. 'I know you prefer girly men.'

I need to pee. I run to their sparkling clean toilet, and pull down my trousers and knickers. While urinating, the image of Zahra's soft skin being cut by a sharp beard passes before my eyes, then I hear Zahra moaning. I abhor my twisted imagination. I try to flush these thoughts down with my urine, but it's impossible. I go back to the kitchen, and gratefully realise she's poured another cup of tea for me.

'So what about you?' Zahra is staring into my eyes with her dark ones, which freakishly resemble my own. 'You were always naughty . . . do you have someone in mind?'

'Oh, god, no,' I hear my mother responding.

'You'll find someone in uni . . . I'm sure,' she consoles me.

'But I don't want to,'

'Oh, you're so westernised!' this is a back-handed compliment, which I despise. All my relatives feel the need to throw this at me on every occasion that I'm not in complete agreement with them. I don't feel westernised, I have never been to the west; I am one hundred percent *Irani;* my favourite poet is Sohrab Sepehri. Zahra's English is better than mine.

We are sipping tea, and Zahra is complaining that she feels I'm not opening up to her like before, even though we've always been close. She says I've changed. She keeps repeating that I've changed and even though she doesn't 'mean to complain' she misses the times when we were children and everything was so 'easy' and there weren't any secrets. I can't defend myself, she's right. I remain silent

45

and reminisce about our childhood days, and a memory comes to me.

We are on a trip: me, my baby brother, Zahra, and our parents. Even though I'm only seven, I know my mother loves my uncle, her brother, and passionately dislikes her sister-in-law. I can't see why she hates her, it'd be like hating a stone. I've heard her many times screeching at my Dad, 'I just can't see why my brother married this *hezbollahi* woman!'

'Perhaps, he got her pregnant!' Dad usually responds, to which both of them burst into a hysterical laughter. I don't understand what's so funny about it. How did my uncle 'get' a woman pregnant when they weren't even married? Doesn't God give children to their parents as a gift for their holy matrimony?

Yet, we're always spending our vacations together. My mother and my uncle are always telling jokes that we don't understand and bursting into celebratory laughter while my uncle's wife and my father uncomfortably smile off into space.

I also noticed Zahra's mum was *chadori* – when we were out, she always wore a black chador, whereas my mother would merely wear a loose satin headscarf – which only made her look prettier and more flamboyant. And when we were inside, she wouldn't even wear that, everyone could see her dark curly hair around her shoulders – a carefree cat lying on a delicate shelf.

When Zahra turned nine, she'd also started wearing a colourful little headscarf on her head, even when we were inside, while her mother was in a floral chador, giving pale smiles to the guests or baking aromatic cinnamon cookies, which my father and I would devour in a blink of an eye. My mother hardly touched the cookies, declaring she was not crazy about getting diabetes.

On this specific trip to the north of Iran on a sizzling summer day, I was wearing my usual blue shorts, ones that I was so attached to I wouldn't even let my parents wash them. They had to wash the shorts in secret while I was asleep. Otherwise, I would've thrown a tantrum. And apparently, nobody could bear my horrid tantrums when I was a child. Sometimes, I wish I still had the same power.

Our cars stop somewhere in the middle of the sweltering road. I jump out of our car to go and socialise with Zahra, and my mother flies out of our car to her brother, who is not driving anymore and is giving us stinky egg sandwiches from a plastic box. Dad stays in the car, drinking tea from his flask, fighting off the exhaustion brought on by the long hours of driving. My uncle brings him an evil-smelling sandwich and forces it on him through the open window with his perpetual smile. Dad accepts the sandwich and smiles back, thanking him warmly, but I see him putting the sandwich in the trash area of the car. He keeps drinking tea out of his sliver flask. For some reason, I don't want to leave him alone in the car, but my desire to play with Zahra defeats all my other wishes. Anyway my dad is carried away with the loud news on the radio as always.

The road is awash with matte grey pebbles. Zahra is also coming out of their car and greets me with her bright smile. I want to whisper in her ears that I think the egg sandwiches smell like fart; I know it would make her laugh.

My uncle's wife is wandering on the road beside the cars,

in her usual black chador, as solemn as ever. My mother has replaced her in the front seat of their car, laughing loudly with her brother. My uncle is biting an egg sandwich while chuckling fondly with his sister. My mother's scarf keeps falling from her head to her shoulders, and she puts it back on each time after a pause. Dad is still drinking from his flask, staring into space, as he usually does while listening to the news. I think of joining my uncle's car for the rest of the commute. I want to travel with Zahra. My parents will listen to the news, and sometimes they discuss it endlessly and loudly, until my younger brother wakes up and weeps. Then they play this dull music they're so fond of. The music is melancholic, I feel the loud strings of the instruments piercing my eardrums, and my parents' favourite singer, Shajarian, keeps saying *Aaaaaaaaaa* in a doleful tone, as though he's being tortured. But I don't say anything, because my mother is shaking her head to the music while singing along, reciting those difficult words. I know it's the same language we speak but I barely understand a word.

I want to be in Zahra's car and talk to her about school. If I'm honest her mother scares me a bit, but I'm too infatuated with Zahra's company to care. Her mother is a shaking ginormous tree that might fall on you, you can see its shadow, but you need not worry, it will never fall.

My uncle can be kind of fun. He gives us *Aidin* fruit candies and makes jokes about our school. Sometimes he asks me whether I like my teacher, and when I say 'I love my teacher.' He tells me not to lie. I know he's joking, but it's still annoying.

And yet Zahra's company is worth it.

Zahra recounts hilarious stuff from her school, and

whispers to me about which one of our relatives is getting married. There's no annoying music in their car. There is no music at all.

Zahra's mother is usually muttering to herself. Zahra says she's praying because she's a very good woman who loves God.

Zahra and I are standing on the side of the road, narrowing our eyes to battle the aggressive sun. Zahra's mother is still wandering about, whispering to herself. I'm starting to think that this woman creeps me out. Perhaps, one day, I'll hate her like my mum does.

My mother is still chatting to her brother in the car. Dad has stopped drinking tea. My brother is awake on his lap. Dad is rubbing his cheeks to my brother's. I feel quite jealous, I want to be the one he's rubbing his cheeks against, and for a moment, I'm almost running back to our car, but Zahra grabs my hand.

'Your dad and my mother should've married each other, don't you think?' I say.

'That's such a disgusting thing to say!' to my utter shock, Zahra growls. 'You're such a child! Well, it's because you're only seven ... not ten, like me.'

'So what?' I retort. 'You're only three years older than me. Zahra, I hate it when you behave like an adult. You're not!' I inform her.

'But you are a child,' Zahra says with a cool smile. 'You don't even wear a headscarf!' Then she glances at my plump thighs in my favourite blue shorts.

'I do at school ...' I inform her.

'Yes, but God is everywhere ... not just at school!'

I'm not sure what she is talking about, yet I'm willing to

leave her company. I look away and see my father kissing my brother on the cheek. I know he will kiss me too if I go back to our car, instead of arguing in the heat with my best friend.

I'm wondering whether to go or stay. Will Zahra stop being so crazy and be her fun self again, or shall I run to my dad already?

Zahra takes both of my hands and catches my eyes. 'You'll be an adult in two years, you'll be old enough to wear a *hejab*. Hazrat-e Fatemeh got married when she was nine. Haven't they taught you this yet?'

'No,' I respond, startled. 'Also, my parents say not to take religious lessons seriously and focus on maths. Still, my maths sucks!'

'Well, no wonder it sucks. I don't think God likes you.'

Now, I really want to go back to our car. I would bear the loud news and the music, I would bear my little brother's shrieks, and my parents spoiling him, I'd even bear my parents arguing about things I don't understand. I just don't want to be with Zahra at the moment. Perhaps I will later, when she's herself again. We'll go to the beach together, we'll swim in the sea pretending we are sisters drowning in an ocean, clinging to each other. We'll make sand castles with my uncle. We will be friends again.

Zahra pulls me closer to her and murmurs in my ear, 'I want to tell you a secret. I've kept it for a while now, but I can't anymore.' At the mention of the word 'secret' I'm good again, excited, I know Zahra will tell me something fun about our older cousins and their crushes on each other.

'My mother says your mother will go to hell when she

dies,' she says, and as if this wasn't horrid enough, she adds, 'and you will too, if you end up dressing like her. For each string of your hair that *namahrams* see, there will grow a snake.'

At first, I think I've heard this wrong, but in a moment I find myself sobbing. As Zahra is shushing me and pleading with me to stay quiet or she'll stop being my friend, my sob turns into a hysterical cry – like the ones my younger brother delivers when he's not getting enough attention. And even though I want to stop it, I can't. It's the thought of my mother's death that's so terrifyingly new to me. And the thought of such horrifying creatures on my head is making my body shake.

At the sound of my cry, Zahra's mother rushes to us, 'what's wrong children?' she asks and gives me a half-hug, 'what's wrong, my dear? Would you like an egg sandwich?' then she looks at Zahra quizzically, while Zahra has zipped her mouth. 'I said, what happened?' she shouts at Zahra as my weeping becomes louder. Zahra finally manages to claim that 'nothing' happened and that I'm just 'spoilt'. They walk back to their car at the precise moment that my mother is getting out of it, running towards me with worried eyes, 'What's wrong, my love?'

Zahra's mother steps away, and my mother hugs me hard. I cry some more in her arms, until my throat burns with dryness.

My mother caresses me, she smells like candy, but I know she doesn't have any candy, it's just her hand cream. 'Do you know what happened?' she's gazing at Zahra's mother.

'No, Zahra said nothing happened,' she replies. She's almost turning to go to their car when I hear myself saying,

'Zahra said you'll die and go to hell, and I'll have snakes on my head because I'm not covering my hair.'

My mother and Zahra's mother look equally shocked, staring at me in disbelief. 'Are you dying?' Zahra is right, my voice sounds really spoilt, but I couldn't care less.

'No, honey, I'm with you! I'm young and healthy.' My mother embraces me so tightly I can't breathe. I feel like taking off my shorts; I'm sweating.

'I will punish Zahra for what she said to you,' Zahra's mother states. My mother stands straight and stares at her again. I've never seen her facial expression so distorted and strange; she looks as though her mouth is filled with stones. 'Don't punish that poor child, instead stop feeding her rubbish!'

Zahra's mother goes pale, but she firmly retorts, 'I'm not even going to argue with you, you're ruining this trip for everyone.'

By this time, my dad is getting out of his car, my brother shining in his arms. 'What's going on? Why are we wasting so much time?' he asks my mother, as though she were the only person around.

'We're not going to *shomal*,' Mum declares, 'Let's go back to Tehran.' Her voice is so hard yet so hysterical my dad doesn't even question her decision. I wonder what Zahra and her cool dad are doing in their car.

We all leave the battlefield in silence, I walk between my parents, both my hands supported by theirs. I'm not sorry we're not going to *shomal*. I'm still a bit unsure as to whether Zahra actually said those weird words or whether I just imagined it all. I feel like having ice cream.

In the car I fall asleep, and sleep all the way back to

Tehran. The car has become quiet, like my uncle's car: no music, no radio, no conversation. Later on, in my dismay, I realise this was our last trip with Zahra. I still get to see her, but only at family gatherings. We don't travel together any longer.

And now Zahra is about to get married. She's an engineer, and like her mother she wears a black chador when she leaves the house and prays five times a day, but she's not taciturn like her. And she's not dead like her. Zahra's mother passed away three years ago from lung cancer. Well, I hope she's in heaven at last.

Tehran *Yaoi*

I fall in love with him the moment he opens the door. There's a surprised silence on both sides, until Maryam introduces me to the most enchanting boy I've ever met.

It's not just his physical beauty that moves me; there's something in his eyes that I urgently need to possess.

I interrogate Maryam under my breath. 'Why haven't you introduced us before?'

'They're all a bit *cheeep*, aren't they? I was hesitant about even bringing you here tonight,' she whispers in my ear. 'You're sublime, darling, I wouldn't introduce you to some *loozer*!'

'But he's not a *loozer*!'

Maryam tilts her glamorous head blowing her Marlboro fumes away from my face. 'But, look at your eyes . . . And I envy your cheekbones!'

I'm aware she's charming me to win the argument and I'm happy to let her. Her compliments make me feel so good, I feel like a god – albeit a fallen one. I look into her navy-shadowed eyes and conclude how fortunate I am to have found a friend like her in a country whose president has denied my existence. I bend and kiss her hand, because sometimes, instead of a godly gay man, I am her grateful little slave.

The beautiful host hands us two glasses of aragh mixed with orange juice, its aggressive taste burning my throat like the semen of a drugged-up lover. I am reluctant to drink it; I've heard stories of bad aragh blinding people. But I smile at my new love, saying, 'This is the best drink I've ever had in my life.'

He smiles back, staring into my eyes with his kohl-rimmed ones. 'I'm glad,' he says, his voice as sweet as his smile.

There are a few other guests, in whom I have no interest. They're talking hysterically, possibly about something dull, like politics – the new protests and conflicts, about who rigged the election and who got arrested.

I sit beside Maryam, murmuring, 'I want him.'

Maryam looks at me in choked surprise. 'He's not that pretty! Also, sorry to shatter the castle of your dreams, darling, but he has a boyfriend.'

'Of course Ahmadinejad cheated, people voted for Mousavi! How dare you question that, after all that's happened?' a girl with dyed blonde hair is screaming at a spotty-faced boy.

'They're probably not exclusive.' I'm trying to hold on to the rubble of my castle. When it comes to sex, I suddenly become an optimistic and hopeful person.

'They are,' Maryam hisses. 'Just go near them to get sick of the stench of their monogamy – although it shouldn't matter to you, as you can seduce anyone anyway.'

I leave Maryam and saunter to the other side of the living

room where our host is showing a black-and-white painting to another boy.

The homemade aragh, which probably is poisoning me, has boosted my self-confidence. 'Oh my God! Who painted this? It's magnificent!' I exclaim.

'I did,' he says, blushing. 'It sucks.'

I grab the painting and gaze at it for a while. I don't really get any of it. It's too modern, too abstract. And as it's black and white, I can't even stick to the traditional way of interpreting colours. Although I can't fathom it, I find myself relishing just looking at it. From afar it was more like elegant scribbling, but looking closely, I can find order in it. He explains it to me and suddenly I understand it. I point out something about the painting and he says passionately, 'You got that? Nobody understood it.' *Well*, I think, *because nobody understands you like I do.*

I try to make other points about the painting, but sadly none of them excites him as much as my first one. I put my head close to his and murmur the points to him, trying my best not to stare at his slender neck and little lips, to look merely immersed in his art and nothing else. He tells me he has more work in his room and if I am interested we can go check them out. Of course I am interested. A room is a personal thing. Very personal, I hope. Also, I can flirt better in his room – away from all the political fervour.

On the way to his room, he takes my left hand loosely, then exclaims, 'Oh, your hands are so soft!'

I smile. 'I take good care of them,' I say, then staring at his, I confess, 'You should take good care of yours, too. You've got absolutely gorgeous hands. Most men's are coarse and hairy.'

He caresses my wrist. 'Oh, you give me so much confidence, *azizam*! But I know what you're saying. I can't stand bad-looking hands, either. Such a turn-off!' While uttering the word *azizam*, his voice becomes so coquettish and nasal that it stretches and rings like ten bells in my excited ears.

His half-dark room smells like the cologne he's wearing: my guess is Hugo Boss. I want to sniff him until I'm incapable of breathing. I want to tell him that his room and neck smell like heaven – if heaven existed. But I don't want to scare him off, so we have the same dialogue about his paintings, only in more detail. 'Although you're drawing the appearances, your aim is to represent the inner parts, am I right?'

He says I'm right, then shows me a work from the time when he was an *'amator'*: a boat on colourful waves, which he retrieves from his closet. I look into his eyes and tell him this one reminds me of Monet. My words are still floating in the air when his boyfriend creeps in, stout, his superfluous breath staining the atmosphere of the room. I notice how thick and hairy his hands are and I am about to point that out and ask, 'But how can you be with him? You just said you can't stand bad hands, and you like mine! Then why are you with him and not with me?' However, I keep my mouth shut and pretend to be drowning in his paintings, even though he is the only thing I'm drowning in. His hands are a work of art in themselves; he doesn't need to create anything. I want to lose myself in the hollows of his cheekbones. I could suck his fingers and lips for hours before putting our exploding cocks in the warmth of each other's mouths. We would be even more beautiful than *yaoi*. Our sacred sex would salvage this horrendous world. But I don't say these words to him, obviously, especially with his boy-friend in the room, whose furious breathing shreds my ears.

'What are you guys doing?' the boyfriend asks with a creepy smile. I notice his teeth are whiter than mine and I feel more defeated than before.

'Fucking.' He bursts out laughing at his own joke. The boyfriend and I exchange uncomfortable smiles. Suddenly, I realise Maryam is right. I'm assailed by the stench of their monogamy: the morning breath, the murdered desires, the slaughtered opportunities, the crippling jealousy, the hateful need, the fabricated conscience. I am on the verge of tears.

'He was just showing me his paintings,' I say, trying not to sound awkward. 'They're extraordinary, aren't they?'

He interrupts his boyfriend's half-formed 'Yes', saying 'He doesn't really care about these things,' and wraps his arms around his boyfriend's shoulders to make his words sound less toxic. The boyfriend merely smiles. I wonder why he doesn't defend himself. I would have defended myself. I would've screamed, 'But I do care about your paintings, darling!'

As the air feels suddenly plumbago dense, I excuse myself and quietly storm out of the room, declaring that I need to pee. I suspect he wants me to compete with his boyfriend, and I am determined not to let that happen; it is just impossible for a horse to compete with a rat. I shall not lower myself by taking part in his childish games. My arms are generously open for him, he can come in my embrace – and my mouth – whenever he wishes.

In his bathroom, instead of pissing, I simply stare into the monstrous mirror above the basin, observing the face that has made my life possible and sometimes even enjoyable. Maryam is absolutely right: I am probably the most gorgeous boy in Tehran, although there are many of us, existing gloriously while our so-called president insists otherwise. But I have no desire to think about his pettiness and nastiness, otherwise I'll end up in tears of rage. I caress my straight, dark hair away from my forehead, and stroke the flawless skin of my high cheekbones. I am pleased about looking like the most beautiful woman in the world, my mother; in almost every way except that I have my father's big mouth – which is unsurprisingly quite popular with men. Although I can never tell my father this, as it might lead to his suicide.

I want to masturbate. I want my semen to ossify around his basin like a bas-relief . . . but I hear my boy calling my name. And I realise I have not wanted anyone like this since I was fifteen, and I have never felt so cheap. I feel trapped and unfortunate. And yet thrilled.

As soon as I step out of the bathroom, I catch him behind the door, a faithful little puppy, yapping, 'Come join us!' We lock eyes, until he averts his to the floor, his delicate face turning bright red.

I don't have the slightest idea why he has changed his white T-shirt with the exquisite image of burning buildings for a black T-shirt that has a horrendous picture of Lady Gaga on it. Perhaps his jealous boyfriend coerced him into sex as soon as I left the room. I regret my impulsive decision to leave them alone.

'You actually like her?' one of the guests asks, pointing at his new shirt, not even waiting for his response. 'She's *so* ugly!' My boy doesn't reply, but his delightful face becomes doleful. I attack the person with my drunken voice, 'Lady

Gaga looks gorgeous . . . but in an unconventional way. Her beauty is unique, it's not for everyone to see.' His dark eyes are shining as he stares at me with admiration.

I continue my lies about Lady Gaga. 'Lady Gaga is a true postmodernist and that's why I love her – she plays with all the boundaries and definitions. She's questioned everything!' I can see that the other person has lost interest in this conversation and is regretting his comment. But my beautiful boy is still nodding his head in acknowledgement.

Maryam is silently laughing at me on the other side of the living room. The boyfriend looks like blank cardboard. He looks invisible.

'Maryam, why didn't you introduce us sooner?' He has put his hands around my shoulders. I feel warm and yet shaky.

'Because she's a vicious witch.' I squeeze his hands and he laughs. So does Maryam. But I can't bear my own sarcasm towards my best friend and blow her a kiss.

She winks at me and says, 'Yes, I should have. You guys do click. I'm almost jealous!'

'You should be!' he says, leaving me to go and sit beside his blank boyfriend.

It's about one in the morning and fortunately most people have left. And those who have remained are restlessly intoxicated, so we start to play a game, and not just any game, the most dangerous game ever: Truth or Dare.

Right before we start spinning the empty aragh bottle, my boy asks us, 'By the way, are you guys going to the rally on Thursday? I think we should go together.' He looks at Maryam and me, and then at the other boy whose unnecessary name escapes my head.

'Sure,' Maryam replies, glancing at me with a worried expression, knowing I am going to protest against her going to the protest.

'Well,' I say, even though there is nothing more romantic than going to a rally against the government, 'to be honest, I'm not going. And you guys shouldn't go either.' Of course, I am only worried about him and Maryam. The nameless boy and the boyfriend are more than welcome to go.

'You mean you don't believe in the Green Movement?' my boy asks, puffing his cigarette forcefully in my face. I want to choke on his smoke. I am slightly hard and dizzy, which makes politics slip away from me. I am lying on a sunny beach and a plane is exploding in the distant sky.

'Of course I do. And I support it. And admire it. I just don't believe it's going to work and change anything other than induce further bloodshed at the hands of the *Basijis*. I'm scared of them. They've always won. They're going to win this time, too.' I try my best to sound detached and cruelly logical, but my voice breaks like a sentimental bastard. I am thrown out of the sunny beach, back to savage politics. I am a homeless child shivering in winter. Because I have also voted for Mousavi in the hope of the slightest change, but I am not going to fight for my moderate vote.

He looks at me in surprise, possibly disillusioned and hurt. I can lie about pop stars, but for some reason I can't lie about my political beliefs. 'I'm scared,' I repeat. 'I don't want to be tortured. I wouldn't be able to stand it. I don't want my parents to die of grief.' I don't admit I'm also horrified at the idea of my perfect features being destroyed by a bunch of beasts whose hands are made of batons. (Sometimes, I find being gorgeous so stressful that I almost wish I were plain.)

The picture of the bloody face of Neda Agha-Soltan flashes before my eyes, the first victim of the rallies, shot by the *Basijis* in the first protest, a few months ago. The government insisted she was a 'spy', shot by 'the enemy'. She was our age, twenty- something. Twenty-seven? I don't remember and I don't want to remember. I can't forget her eyes, though, no matter how hard I try. Because even though she was dead, they remained open. They were wide and terribly beautiful. I think she had some mascara on her long eyelashes. That's why I don't think she expected to die. After all, it was supposed to be a 'peaceful' protest. I don't imagine she expected to get shot. She just wanted her vote. An honest election. A moderate president. Nobody extraordinary, nobody outside the system.

In my darkest dreams, where I can be as much of a jerk as I please, I ask her, 'Neda, was it worth it?'

She scoffs, 'Can't you see the blood on my lifeless face?'

It is the only thing I can see, in fact it has haunted my nightmares, but I don't tell her that, because she already sounds angry. She is especially mad at me – in the way that all self-sacrificing people are mad at selfish people. And I wonder if the only real war is between sacrifice and self-interest.

His beauty wanes for a moment, like the moon behind clouds. Like the sacrifice of the martyrs behind the selfishness of the living.

He sips his aragh and orange juice and smiles dreamily, cigaretteless. 'You know, sometimes I find myself fancying those *Basijis* . . . They're so unapologetically manly, so masculine in the most animalistic way.'

'Stop!' I feel nauseous. Now I am certain that my delicate

63

physique is not his type. My skin is too soft for him, my hair too long, my nails too neat. He is into stinky gorillas who wouldn't even look at his paintings, let alone admire every shade of his neck. In short, I am a magnolia and he is into cacti. I am a horse, but he likes rats. And he probably thinks I'm a masochistic 'bot'. I am aching to inform him that I'd be great at fucking his toned bum. I feel it is my moral duty to inform him I fuck in the most 'animalistic' way possible – harder than the *Basijis*. 'Can we forget about politics for a second and start our game? It's getting late. I want to have fun.'

He smiles at me and spins the bottle. I feel upset and grateful that he is still smiling at me, not judging me for my cowardice. I wonder if we will ever be such close friends that I could honestly tell him I can't wait to leave this bleeding country, that I have already received an admission offer from a foreign university in a fairly peaceful place. Because I am done. I am a leaver. A coward. A liar. A sinner. *Can you still smile at me and show me your paintings?*

I can't enjoy the game. I'm getting more and more nervous. He is French kissing his boyfriend. And for the very first time in my life, the sight of two boys kissing makes me feel ill, as though they were some hideous straight couple. I want him to sit beside me and break up with his quiet boyfriend and stop fancying bearded *Basijis* at once, without any fuss; like a scenario that has been written beforehand. I want everything to go smoothly. I don't want to play games any more. I don't want to express any more political opinions, or any opinions at all for that matter. I don't wish to defend anything anymore – even myself and my beliefs, let alone Lady fucking Gaga and my fucked-up country. I just want him to leave his boyfriend quietly and come to me. But he does not do that; because sadly enough I am not God. And nothing goes according to my will. In fact, everything goes in the opposite direction, as if everything aims to destroy me. I tell them to stop and that they are ruining the game. They obediently stop. But the boyfriend is still touching him – although I don't blame him. I would do the same. I understand him as a person, but abhor him as an obstacle.

'When was the last time you had sex?' nameless asks me. I'm happy; he is not so useless, after all. This is an opportunity for me to make my boy jealous. Without hesitation, I gloriously lie, 'This morning.'

'With whom?' my boy asks jealously.

'It's not your turn to ask.' The boring boyfriend reminds us that we have to follow the rules, but Maryam defies him. 'No, tell us! I'm turned on!'

I stare at my boy. I am almost certain he will be mine; it's just a matter of time. 'With a very beautiful boy called Ehsan. Hunted him from manjam.com.'

'Are you in love with him?' His questions are starting to sound pathetically forward. I'm bursting with happiness. My boy will be desperate for me.

'Not really. He's boring. He's an engineer.'

He breaks into hysterical laughter. Maryam also laughs – but it is a different laugh, it's the laughter of victory, reassuring me we will win.

The bottle orders his boyfriend to ask me a question. I'm preparing myself for a war. But he only asks how old I am. I tell the truth for the first time – there's nothing to hide about youth: twenty-three.

My love comments again. 'You're two years older than me!'
'Yes,' I say, teasing, 'that's why you have to respect me!'
'Never!' he chuckles, his mouth open, ready to devour me.

I play an old trick that never fails. I steal his pack of cigarettes. 'You have to come get it,' I invite him when he asks
me to light him one. He joyously accepts this challenge,
leaves the boyfriend and dives on me. I am lying on the
carpeted floor and he is lying on me, I am crushing the pack
of cigarettes in my tight fist while gazing hard into his eyes,
whispering, 'You can't get it,' and he does not even pretend
to be annoyed, instead swings his deliciously sweaty body
on top of me, guffawing ferociously, scratching my hand
like a bewildered cat under the pretext of reaching for his
pack. I am aware the old trick is working; once they come
into close contact with my skin, my stare, my scent, they
are not able to resist. At times, they even go insane. But
with him, it's not just sex. I want to reach him. I want to
have him. And considering the way he is panting on top of
me, rolling all over me, I can tell he wants it too. I can see
betrayal in his eyes and it is beautiful.

My ecstasy is intensified when I hear Maryam saying,
'This is gorgeous . . . I'd like to photograph you two sometime . . .' I laugh at the lovely thought that my charming
Maryam, my sweet saviour, has already written the script.
A photography session in her strangely lit gallery does
sound perfect. I imagine her, gloriously tall in her leather
high heels, charmingly disdainful and shamelessly aroused,
pointing her Canon lens at us like a loaded shotgun, com-
manding us to touch each other – for the sake of art, of
course. And who are we, mere mortals, to disobey the
bloodthirsty goddess of photography?

My surreptitiously erect cock goes flaccid as I hear the irrelevant voice of the boyfriend begging him, 'Come here, sweetheart, smoke my cigarettes.' My clenched fist opens and the lifeless pack of cigarettes falls to the floor. He has already left me.

And the bottle is still spinning, like my head.

Without much thinking, I dare him to lick anyone's fingers – except his boyfriend's. He tells me to offer him mine and he licks each finger of my right hand, and life becomes sweet. Now my ruthless penis is as restless as me.

I cannot look at him.

I just observe how I lose the game while his boyfriend wins. Like how I lost my country to the *Basijis*. And yet I don't want losing to become a habit.

This time he picks truth. I hear Maryam asking him if he would date me if he were single.

'Well, he's stunning!' he says, giggling. 'Too bad I'm in love!'

I feel like crying in a dark corner while coming up with a plan to annihilate his rotten relationship. But instead I try to play along. 'What if I were a straight man?'

'Come on, I'd seduce you,' he stares at me, his eyes deep and dark like my fantasies. 'Believe me, I could.' I have no doubt about that.

The boyfriend smiles at me and wraps his hairy arms around my boy's shoulders. 'You're so naughty!' This is his first and hopefully last comment of the party.

'I have to go. I have a class tomorrow,' I lie. 'It was nice meeting you all.' Another lie. It was destructive to meet you. I just want to go home and die. Or maybe just cry. Or listen to music, alone, in the dark.

'But I was hoping you could stay the night here and play till morning,' he says. 'It's just getting more interesting. Please, stay. Please!' I wonder how on earth I can find the power to reject him.

'Actually, I have to leave, too,' Maryam rescues me as always. 'Let's go together.' She takes my hand. The warmth and strength of her grip soothe me.

'I won't insist, then. But let's catch up soon. Okay?' He playfully gazes at me. 'Of course, if we don't get arrested on Thursday.' His giggle pierces my eardrums. I need to vomit.

'Just don't go,' I blurt out. 'Actually, I'm throwing a party on Thursday. You guys should come.' I look at his boyfriend as though he were my main guest, the life of my party.

'Thanks! I'll try to make it.' The boyfriend shakes my hand and smiles. I feel bad that he is so polite and decent. So quiet and unruffled. So much the opposite of me.

I don't even look at my boy while saying goodbye. Instead I look at his boyfriend and miserably smile. He has put his confident arms around my property, my land, as if it were really his.

The way he looks at me from his boyfriend's arms is like throwing a lit match on the gasoline racing through my veins.

I feel fire invading my cells. But even fire cannot make a fighter out of me. I am already thinking of excuses to cancel my fake party. Maryam is going to the rally anyway. I shall stay home – preferably in my room – and distract myself by gathering those endless documents for my visa application while avoiding the news in the foolish hope of burying my worries about Maryam, my parents, and everyone else. And I shall masturbate in the dark, under my lilac sheets – not in front of my tall mirror, nor over *yaoi* any more – with his image carved in my mind like the sweetest sculpture that can also speak and say, 'Stay, please.'

I am not fighting for anyone. I am not fighting for you. I do not fight for my land. Because, my love, I believe nothing is worth fighting for. Not the election, not our country, and not even you and your perfect hands.

Soho

I'm about to fall on the ground in Dean Street, but I hold on to a construction fence to steady myself. My scarf has turned into a snake again, choking me. I would love to collapse on the ground and fall into an everlasting coma, but people are already staring at me, some asking if I'm 'all right' – to which I aggressively turn my head so they will leave me alone.

I know it must be around ten in the morning: the spring sun is sprinkling on London, the day hideously stunning. Even though I am wearing my enormous sunglasses, I can still feel the glory of London and the decadence of Europe seducing me. The fast cars of Soho pass by me and I consider throwing myself under one of them – preferably a blood-red Lamborghini. But what if I survive the accident, stuck in a wheelchair, with my test results in my left hand? Like I was taught in my elementary school: that is the hand with which the sinners will hold the record of their deeds on the Judgement Day.

I am a sinner. I deserve to be judged and thrown into hell. Even though, until two days ago, I thought I was a liberated atheist. But who was I fooling?

I have slept with thirteen men since my arrival in England two years ago. Thirteen is an ominous number in our ancient culture. I used to think it was under ten men, but last night I stayed awake, not caring about getting my beauty sleep anymore, counting, focusing, regretting. Not missing anyone: Steven, John, James, Liam, Stephen, Babatunde, Josh ... and I do not remember all the other names, but I recall their faces.

The only person I've confided in about my fear is my only Iranian friend in London. She was not surprised at my shameful secret, because she had been suffering from the exact same fear until she entered a monogamous relationship with a dull old man. She told me not to worry and added, 'Your disease isn't AIDS. It's immigration.'

I laughed insultingly at this accusation and attacked her by saying, 'I'm not like you. I adore Europe. I've worked really hard to get here. My mother is still angry that I've left Iran on my own – husbandless.'

My mother. The God-lover. The history professor. At times, a bigger dictator than Iran's Supreme Leader, screaming at my dad for spoiling me and raising me as a non-religious person; at times praising us, even cooking for us the finest *zereshk polo* with saffroned chicken marinated in lemon juice overnight. My mother, with her scary prophecies. The last one happened the night before I was leaving the country.

My father and I were in my orange-lit room, packing, me worrying about the lack of space and my father reassuring me that he could squeeze everything into my suitcase. Suddenly, I noticed how old his hands looked, and

I couldn't take it anymore. The tears I'd fought since that morning streamed down my face. 'I don't want to leave without you,' I confessed.

My father looked up from the suitcase; a pair of red sandals fell from his hands. 'I'll come and visit you, I promise. And you'll come back in the holidays.'

I managed a tearful smile and my father left my room. I knew my drama was too much for him, but I couldn't help it. I knew he was going to the balcony to smoke and choke on his tears. Then my mother stepped into my room. I was still weeping into my overflowing suitcase, forcing a volume of Forough Farrokhzad's poetry amidst my shoes.

'You should be celebrating tonight!' my mother declared. 'You finally got what you wanted, with the help of your beloved father.'

For the first time in my life, I was completely honest with her. 'I can't leave him.'

Then my mother did something strange: she embraced me and caressed my head, like she did when I was a child and we weren't shouting at each other about religion the whole time.

'Have the strength to accept what you strived for. This is also what your father wants for you. Don't worry about him. I'll take care of him.'

My tears finally stopped. I looked at her and said, 'I'm glad you're finally supporting my decision.'

'I still think you'll be disillusioned,' she said, her dark eyes glued to mine. 'Europe isn't as perfect as the utopia in your head.'

'Nowhere is,' I reasoned, 'but it's definitely better than here.'

'Your problem is you are more westernised than the West itself,' she said. 'You won't find peace there. Somebody with your attitudes should go to live on Mars!'

How can I tell this lioness what I have done to her daughter's body?

I even know who gave it to me. It was John. A long-haired boy doing a PhD in war studies and video games, or something as absurd as that. John was living in Cockfosters with his parents, whom I never had the honour of meeting in person. He was so gorgeous that, whenever we went out, men would look at him more than they'd look at me. He was abnormally bony though, and he was into BDSM and sex parties – which at that time, I considered to be a symbol of liberation and pleasure, but now I fear like death itself.

My vagina has started itching since he performed cunnilingus on me thirteen months ago. The worst part is that I didn't even come, because his teeth were too sharp, scrubbing my clitoris like a nail buffer. After our unsexy sex, John vanished. He didn't reply to my myriad text messages asking whether he had an STD and then he deactivated his online dating profile.

Once John left me with an itchy vagina, I became weaker by the day. Even now, today, as I am walking in my sacred Soho, I feel like I need physical help. I can't even walk. I am also losing my looks; my once lively eyes look lifeless, encircled by brownish shadows. Strands of my hair are falling as often as the London rain. My cheekbones are becoming hollower by the second. I look like a victim of

AIDS, and get confused – and even upset – when people say I look 'beautiful'.

After mocking all my religious teachers for ten years and longing to escape to my fantastical Europe, now I am almost certain those *chadori* teachers were right: Europe is HIV positive.

I am now walking as slowly as I can, hoping I will not find the clinic. They will test you for free. These past few weeks, I found myself crying under my red duvet, not leaving my room the whole day even though I was invited to a few parties. Yesterday, I almost missed a lecture. And when I finally made it, three of my classmates asked me worriedly, 'Why do you look so tired?'

My gums have started bleeding whenever I brush my teeth. I Googled it, and apparently it is one of the symptoms of either AIDS or diabetes. I have been tested for diabetes a hundred times. Unfortunately, I don't have it.

The tragi-comic part of my story is that after sleeping with numerous men, I've reached the conclusion that I'm not even into men – perhaps this explains why they're incapable of giving me orgasms and why I can't fall in love with them. I mostly fall in love with women, even though I haven't had the confidence to actually sleep with them. This is the ultimate absurdity: I am an AIDS-stricken lesbian. Good luck to me explaining *that* to my mother.

I should be in the library now, underlining *Orientalism*; instead, I'm crawling to the sordid clinic taking deep breaths with a choking sound because I can't really breathe, because I don't know how to inform my parents of my disgraceful disease. They've sent me to England to prosper; instead I have destroyed myself with sex.

But I'll finally find the courage to tell them.

After all, my mother did tell me once that I look like *'viroos-e-AIDS'* after finding out I was not a virgin. But that was ages ago. I was eighteen. She's apologised a few times since. But it was a prophecy. I know my clever mother was right. I am a human immunodeficiency virus.

Soho is crumbling before my eyes. I do not fancy Europe any more. Every English novel I read is filled with gay characters who end up being diagnosed with AIDS – my all-time favourite novel, Alan Hollinghurst's *The Line of Beauty*, is just one example. In London, on all the walls, there are hysterically happy advertisements of being tested for HIV 'for free!' And I have avoided getting tested for more than a year. But I cannot take it any longer. I might need treatment. Perhaps, instead of paying my over-priced tuition fees, I need to spend this money to prolong the numbered days of my miserable life. But how can I tell my father what I am spending his hard-earned cash on?

I have finally arrived: 34 Dean Street. Unfortunately, I have found the clinic. A guillotine awaits me. This will not be a glorious death, but a disgraceful one. And I will bury the reason. I have already planned my suicide. It will happen this summer in Tehran, on the last day of being with my family. I will throw myself out of my bedroom window – we live on the eighteenth floor, so hopefully I shall be dead, not wheelchaired. I won't leave a suicide note.

The clinic is too bright, so I don't take off my H&M sunglasses; also, I don't want the tattooed receptionist to see the pathetic tears in my eyes.

Liam had extensive tattoos. I picked him up in Camden Town, blinded by his golden locks brightening up the Camden sky. We flirted under the guise of discussing the Arctic Monkeys' discography until the silver London rain started to fall. I offered him my black umbrella. He accepted it and stood beside me. I touched his thin waist under my wet umbrella. We kissed near Camden Lock, his mouth small and minty; I invited him back to my place.

Tattooed people are more likely to be HIV positive. Where did I glean this helpful piece of information?

'Good morning!' the receptionist blurts out.

'He–llo!' I reply joyously – a sad imitation of the good old days when I was young and healthy and seductive. I force a smile that I know is dripping with sickness.

I fill out the form on the computer. It is asking whether I've fucked a bisexual man or not. I think hard. How the hell am I supposed to know the sexual orientation of people whose names I have difficulty recalling?

Yes, on a few occasions, the Boots condoms were torn . . . but that does not count as 'unprotected sex' – or does it?

The happy receptionist asks me to go downstairs and wait for my name to be called.

I crawl down the serpentine staircase and find myself in a black and white room with three beautiful men. Their long legs fidget in sable and purple skinny jeans like the tantalising promise of hell. I ogle their sophisticated buns and anxious eyes. We give each other consoling smiles, regretting our self-sabotaging beauty.

In a few minutes, a tall woman saunters to the waiting room and calls my name.

I run after her like a shot puppy.

We enter a narrow corridor, which I hope is an endless tunnel, but in a moment she opens a door and I find myself in a sunny office with a small, white sink. I throw my body on the sink, my head hanging from my neck like the corpse of the puppy from a tree, and my mouth is a deep well uttering whiny noises like 'aaaaahhhhh' and then, calling the God I was proud of not worshipping, '*khodaaa*'. The woman stares at me, wildly mascaraed eyes wide with discomfort; her tone is cold and almost offended. 'What's wrong?'

Realising she is extraordinarily gorgeous, I'm convinced she is the angel of death. I sit opposite her, feeling small – I am a sacrificed lamb at the altar of the goddess of death.

'Are you okay?'

'No,' I bellow. 'I think I might have AIDS.'

'Why do you think that? Do you have any symptoms?'

'No.' I find myself lying, not being able to tell her about my itchy vagina, bleeding gums, and hair loss.

'Are you a sex worker?' she asks.

'No!' I reply, shaking. 'I'm a student!' I think of my father, who claims to be proud of me. Should he be? I am shedding tears. I haven't seen him in a year, and now the child the old man is proud of has a self-inflicted disease. Instead of a successful doctor, I'll just be a dead student. 'Why are you so worried? Have you had unprotected sex with drug addicts?'

'No!'

'Then why are you so anxious? If you don't tell me, I can't help you.'

'I have slept with thirteen men,' I finally confess to the uninterested goddess.

'That doesn't mean you have AIDS.' I am starting to feel

a bit hopeful, but she adds, 'Also, HIV isn't a death sentence. People live with it until they're eighty, ninety years old.'

I have much difficulty tolerating the mental image of my ninety-year-old HIV-positive self. 'How long will it take?' I ask aggressively. 'Sixty seconds?'

'I'm not going to do the sixty-second test with you. We'll text you the result in six hours. You're not high risk. Also, I won't be able to deal with you if it's a false positive.'

'Six hours?' I scream. But she acts deaf.

My body trembles while she is taking my blood. But as soon as I see the red filling the plastic tube, I feel relieved. My blood looks so pure it shines.

'I'm sorry I behaved a bit dramatically earlier. I'm usually very well-mannered,' I say to the woman, sounding even more insane as I am apologising to her while trying to convince her that I am 'well-mannered'.

'It's all right,' she mutters.

I can feel she can't wait to get rid of me, but I want to stick to her for the rest of my life. I'm considering ways of convincing her to become my carer if I happen to be HIV positive. But she is already kicking me out of her office. I crawl back to my room, not being able to eat lunch, awaiting the fateful text message.

When I reach my bed, I fall unconscious, having the same nightmare that I've had for the last eight months or so: I'm informed that I am HIV positive. I am in the same room with my mother, and when I finally manage to tell her, she just says, 'I knew,' and exits the claustrophobic room, leaving me behind with the test results in my left hand.

My phone vibrates, and I wake up from this charming

dream. *Your HIV test was negative (clear). Your syphilis test was negative (clear). You do not need any treatment.*

My heart pounds hard. I take a deep breath and feel like a newborn, until it occurs to me that the girl is too angelic to let me know the *real* result. She knows I can't handle the truth and would kill myself, hence she has sent me this life-giving lie.

I know I have it. I look in the mirror and examine the pale face my numerous lovers have admired, and it looks like nothing but a true human immunodeficiency virus.

Threesome

When her mobile rang, Kiana already knew who it was, so she threw the essay she was reading on the nearest table, and answered her phone.

'My darling Sayeh, how are you?' Kiana said. But before Sayeh responded, Kiana heard a roaring in the background. Kiana knew it was Sayeh's girlfriend, Asal.

'Can you hear that?' Sayeh said, sobbing.

'Yes,' Kiana mumbled. 'Come over, I'm home.'

Half an hour later Sayeh was on Kiana's bed, tearfully rolling a joint. Her face was more sallow than usual, and her cheekbones sharper. Kiana often envied Sayeh's cheekbones and wished her face was less round and had better bone structure.

'What happened?' Kiana asked, as she went to the kitchen to make tea.

Sayeh followed her to the sun-lit kitchen: 'same old shit.'

'She's paranoid you're cheating?'

'Yes,' Sayeh said, bursting into tears. 'I'm so tired of it.'

Kiana hugged Sayeh so tight she could feel her delicate bones poking into her shoulders; she pressed her even harder. She wanted her cousin to be happy. Kiana was an only child, and her cousin had always been like a sister to her. Seeing Sayeh so upset made her tearful too.

'Have you eaten?' Kiana asked her, opening the door to a half-empty fridge.

Sayeh smiled, 'Not really, Asal is too angry to cook!'

Kiana took out a purplish red onion, minced meat, and a big potato from the fridge. Then she said, 'And you're still too lazy to learn?'

They both chuckled.

'Where's Aunt Nasrin? Where's your dad?'

'At work,' Kiana said, 'it's only 11:30 in the morning.'

'Can I stay over tonight?' Sayeh stared into Kiana's eyes.

Kiana noticed her cousin's eyeliner was smudging her cheeks. Since they were teenagers, Sayeh had been testing new eyeliners, and they were always black. Kiana remembered once she'd asked her why she didn't experiment with more colourful eyeliners, like blues and even reds. Sayeh hadn't even responded, just looked at her like she was the most clueless person on the planet.

'Of course!' Kiana was pleased, she loved having her cousin sleep over: it was reminiscent of the most fun nights of her childhood. She took a wooden board from the side of the kitchen sink, skinned the potato and grated it.

'What are you cooking?' Sayeh asked.

'*Kotlet*,' Kiana said, peeling the onion.

'Yes!' Sayeh smiled so broadly Kiana could count her straight, white teeth. 'Your *kotlet* always improves the situation!'

Chopping the onion, Kiana noticed Sayeh's large eyes were suddenly red and teary. 'Oh, my darling! Are you okay?'

'It's just the onion!' Sayeh sniffed. 'Do you need help?'

'No, it will be faster if I do it myself.'

Kiana put meat, grated potato, and finely-chopped onion in a bowl and broke an egg on top. Then she seasoned it with salt, pepper, and turmeric and mixed them all together.

Looking at the bowl in fascination, Sayeh said, 'Perhaps we should've just ordered pizza!'

Kiana chuckled, 'my god, your laziness!'

Sayeh laughed too and Kiana was relieved that her cousin didn't seem to be upset anymore.

Kiana put the big plate of *kotlet* on the table. Sayeh's eyes twinkled and she took one and blew on it before putting it in her mouth, making happy noises.

Kiana warned her not to burn herself. Then she took out a bottle of *sharab,* poured two glasses and put them on the table.

'Won't your exams start next week?' Sayeh asked, her eyes shining again with joy.

'I've been studying the whole morning for my first pharmacy exam next week.'

'You'll be fine!' Sayeh took a big gulp from her wine. 'My god, your dad's *sharab* is excellent! It's like medicine.'

'Good homemade wine *is* medicinal, according to Avicenna.' Kiana refilled their glasses.

'Oh, thank god,' Sayeh laughed, 'I was worried about my health.'

Kiana put more *kotlets* in Sayeh's plate, asking, 'what shall we have for dessert?'

'Weed.'

After putting the dirty dishes into the dishwasher, they went to Kiana's bedroom. Sayeh threw herself on Kiana's bed, and moaned, 'Why is your room always so tidy?'

Kiana laughed, taking pride in her tidiness. She pulled out her chair from beneath her desk and placed it opposite the bed, so she could look at Sayeh like a professional therapist. Sayeh shoved her small head into Kiana's soft pillow. 'I just want to disappear!'

Kiana just listened. She knew she didn't need to ask anything for Sayeh to give her the whole story.

Sayeh rolled on her back and stared at the ceiling, 'I'm sick of it!'

'Why don't you leave?' Kiana asked, concerned.

'I'm in love with her.'

Kiana knew this. In fact, she didn't want her cousin to leave Asal. She loved Asal, and in her eyes they were such a beautiful, perfect couple. They had fought to be together, and Kiana was proud to be part of their lives, admiring, being admired by them in return. She had accompanied them to all their intense family gatherings, and she knew that they loved her for being such a great ally. Asal, a theatre actor, invited Kiana along to all the top, artsy parties. Kiana hardly had time to hang out with the tedious pharmacy geeks from her university, because she spent her free time with interesting, exciting artists. She was hoping soon she could find an exciting boyfriend or girlfriend. Sometimes she thought if she studied less, she would find someone. But she couldn't help it: she loved pharmacology almost as much as she loved Sayeh and Asal.

And now this was the third afternoon in a row where Sayeh was shoving her head onto her pillow, howling. Kiana felt helpless. She just couldn't fathom how two people as fabulous, talented, and beautiful as Sayeh and Asal had all these issues.

'So, tell me,' Kiana said, staring at Sayeh who was smoking the joint. 'Is it the same problem as yesterday and the day before?'

'I mean,' Sayeh coughed, 'It's always the same issue: she's crazy. Theatre people, my god! Also, who would cheat on a shooting medallist?' Sayeh roared with laughter.

Kiana laughed, but without feeling the joke. Actually, she was impressed by the fact that Asal had a gold medal in shooting. 'It's quite odd that she's so obsessed with this non-issue.' Suddenly, the most urgent matter in the room was to solve the enigma of her cousin's important relationship.

Sayeh passed on the joint to her. Kiana refused it. She just wanted the story. She was already tipsy on her father's homemade wine. Her parents wouldn't be too happy knowing she had started drinking so early on a weekday. They would interrogate her for not being in the library, preparing for her exams.

'She's convinced I'm fucking around,' Sayeh's eyes were tearful again. 'Why would I betray her? I am madly in love with her! I fought with my family to be with her! I've never loved anyone so much in my whole life!' Then she raised her voice, 'Why the hell would I cheat on her? She's everything. She's clever, she's gorgeous, she's successful!'

'Exactly.' Kiana wished she could understand why Asal, who was always kind to her, accused her lovely cousin of such unkind, untrue things. Kiana was wondering how to give more helpful advice to her cousin, when Sayeh's pocket started ringing. Sayeh sat on the bed and reached for her phone, 'shit, it's Asal!' She squeezed her joint in the crystal ashtray by the bed and accepted the call. Asal's voice filled the room like a solemnly beautiful piece of music. 'I can see you're at Kiana's.'

Sayeh turned the phone in Kiana's direction.

'*Salam*,' she blurted excitedly to the iPhone screen. Asal told her she looked 'well' whilst bestowing on her a kind smile. Kiana noticed her eyes were red and puffy.

As Kiana was giving the exact date of her exams to Asal, Sayeh turned the phone towards her own face, saying, 'Look, I don't wanna fight with you.'

'Me neither!' Kiana heard Asal bursting into tears.

'I worship you,' Sayeh said to the camera, 'I'm in love with you. Why would I even touch anybody else when you are so gorgeous and talented? Everybody else looks like a piece of shit compared to you. You're my life.' After saying this, Sayeh also burst into tears.

'Come home,' Asal muttered.

Kiana felt a wave of relief. Asal did not need to torture herself and her cousin. They had such a beautiful love. It would've been ideal if Asal weren't being so crazy.

When Sayeh left, it was almost four in the afternoon and Kiana had a class at eight the next morning. Plus, her parents would be home soon and even though they also loved Sayeh, they were worried she'd distract Kiana from her studies. As long as Kiana remembered, this had been the conflict between them.

She remembered when she was seven years old, she had gone to Sayeh's parents' house in Yousef Abad; after dinner she had gone to Sayeh's room where Sayeh had shown her a collection of fancy erasers and made her laugh by impersonating her teachers. When Kiana's parents informed her they had to leave, she started yelling and crying, saying that as her parents wouldn't give her a sister, she wanted to stay the night in Sayeh's room, playing till morning. Her parents seemed shocked and ashamed. But they laughed alongside Sayeh's parents, saying, 'tomorrow is a school day, if you come home with us tonight, we'll bring you back to Sayeh's tomorrow night, and then you can stay over because the day after tomorrow is Friday!'

Kiana fell for this promise but in the car, her mother told her not to embarrass them ever again in front of other people, and her father told her, the only way she was ever allowed to be absent from school was if she got 'very very very sick, god forbid.' That Friday, her parents took her to the park nearby and bought her coned ice-cream, but it was no fun because Sayeh wasn't there. Kiana remembered that Friday as being one of the saddest and loneliest days of her life.

Kiana put her chair back where it belonged and resumed reading the essay for her class. When her parents arrived home from work, she told them Sayeh had been there for lunch.

'I wish you'd left some *kotlet* for us too!' her father groaned.

Her mother laughed and said, 'how was she?'

'Not very well,' Kiana confessed.

'Oh, why?' Her mother asked, 'Did Asal tell her father about them?' She didn't wait for Kiana to answer, 'You know I was thinking, I can tell him and talk to him about it.'

'Oh no, she told him ages ago!' Kiana retorted, 'he's absolutely fine with it, he'd guessed anyway.'

'Thank god,' her mother responded. 'I met him once, he did seem like a lovely person. Poor guy! Perhaps, we should find him a wife.'

'Oh, mum, please stop!' Kiana said, disliking her mother for always wanting to be the saviour, without actually saving anybody. By this point, her father's TV was so loud that Kiana went to her bedroom and shut the door, feeling annoyed and alone.

Two days after Kiana's exams, it was Asal's twenty-sixth birthday party. Kiana felt lucky she was done with studying for a while, so she could go and enjoy herself. She went to Tandis mall with her mother to purchase a fancy dress, but she realised that she wanted to wear loose trousers with a flannel shirt, just to look cooler and to fit in better with Asal's and Kiana's artsy queer friends. Her mother agreed that the black trousers and the red flannel shirt would be much chicer than a generic dress. Kiana was secretly hoping she could also fall for a woman for the first time and experiment.

The party was in Asal's and Sayeh's shared flat in a tree-lined alley in Tavanir. Kiana loved that area: it was classy and quiet, unlike their area in the north of Tehran, which was full of newly-rich people showing off their pretentious

Porsches. Kiana fantasised about renting a small place on her own in the same district after her graduation. But she was aware her parents had other plans. They wanted her to leave Iran and get another degree from a prestigious Western university. This idea also appealed to her, especially because Sayeh occasionally stated she and Asal wanted to leave Iran in order to officialise their relationship, and that she wanted to get published outside of Iran, because she wanted to write *lezbian* stories instead of teaching English at an institute and having an anonymous – albeit famous – blog in Farsi. Kiana knew Asal was slightly torn about this, as she didn't want to leave her old widowed father.

Kiana didn't know what present to get for Asal. When her mother suggested fancy scented candles from the mall, she felt like hitting her. They ended up in an antique shop in Bazar Tajrish and Kiana managed to find an exquisite crystal rose. She imagined the rose on Asal's and Sayeh's wooden shelf, beside their other shiny objects, a sign of their everlasting love; hopefully it would bring enough security to Asal's crazy head that she would stop shouting at Kiana's vulnerable and innocent cousin about nothing. Why couldn't Asal see that they were ideal? That they were the icons that the society badly needed?

As Kiana approached their flat, she heard Asal's mournful Japanese traditional music echoing in the hallway. Even though she usually appreciated Asal's unusual taste in music, she was slightly annoyed; she wanted to be happy at Asal's birthday party.

Asal opened the door and embraced her warmly. She was wearing a blue velvet dress with matching lipstick. Kiana decided that she was probably the only person on earth who could pull off such a lip colour. She felt underdressed in her ridiculous trousers, but Asal blurted, 'Your shirt is gorgeous! Red suits you so much!'

Kiana handed her the wrapped crystal rose. Sayeh emerged in the living room, in a little black dress, and Kiana noticed she had replaced her usual black eyeliner with a lot of silver shadow: her enormous eyes were two dark moons in her slender face. Sayeh and Asal were both the same height, and it was impossible for Kiana to say which one of them looked more stunning.

Sayeh put her arms around Kiana, saying, 'I see you wanna score tonight,' and winking. Asal said, 'I'm sure you will, my dear. Sorry I asked you to come earlier so we can have a moment to ourselves, but your choices will arrive soon!'

Kiana felt hot and giggled; she loved being part of 'ourselves' and for her 'choices' to arrive later. She brought out the bottle of wine from her bag and handed it to Asal. 'A small present from my parents!'

'Your parents are the best!' Asal declared, pouring from the bottle into three empty glasses on the table.

'*Salamati!*' They clinked their glasses together and Kiana finally felt her body relax after a week of difficult exams. The solemn music changed into joyous K–pop. Kiana was happy to see Asal and Sayeh kissing each other on the lips. The doorbell rang and more guests arrived. The music was so loud, Kiana had difficulty hearing the names of the guests. She was just waiting for the right person. She knew Asal and Sayeh were going to set her up with someone, preferably with a woman.

Even though there weren't many guests, the tiny flat was packed. 'Only special people', Kiana recalled Asal's Facebook invitation and smiled into space, letting her cousin refill her glass, losing count of how many glasses she'd already downed; she was too relaxed and happy to care. So far nobody had attracted her attention, apart from a long-haired boy with beautiful kohl-rimmed eyes who kept smiling at her.

Sayeh was cutting the birthday cake with a long, sharp knife, and Kiana knew her cousin had specifically purchased Asal's favourite: BiBi's chocolate cake. She knew this was only one of Asal's surprises amongst several others, including plane tickets to Phuket, and Sayeh's handmade book of poems about Asal and their love. But why was Asal still so ungrateful? What else did she want? Kiana knew her cousin would die for this woman, why couldn't she see it? Sayeh handed her a saucer of chocolate cake, and Kiana wolfed it down in less than thirty seconds. Asal had good taste: the perfect sweetness of the cake accentuated the aftertaste of the wine in Kiana's mouth. Sayeh grabbed her hand, 'Why are you on your own, my dear cousin? Let's dance!'

Kiana couldn't imagine being anywhere better than dancing with Sayeh in her magnificent flat. Sayeh had her sweet smile and was asking her in a gleeful, shouted whisper if she fancied anybody, to which Kiana could only respond by giggling. Asal interrupted them by saying, 'Some family love, I see,' and separated them to throw her tongue into Sayeh's mouth.

Kiana was slightly annoyed by this, finding Asal's behaviour unnecessarily jealous, possessive, and even dominant. Maybe her cousin was right. Maybe Asal was a little bit crazy after all. While thinking these thoughts, Asal came up to her and gave her a hug, saying, 'I just opened your present! I adore it!' Kissing her cheeks, she continued, 'You do know your friendship is the best gift though!'

Kiana was suddenly so touched she didn't know what to say, so she just embraced Asal again, and said, 'Happy birthday, my gorgeous Asal!' and felt guilty for thinking ill of her seconds ago. By this point Kiana was too drunk to think about her words before uttering them; she heard herself saying, 'You need to be sure that my cousin is in love with you!'

Asal stared at her, her eyes suddenly doleful, 'I know darling, I know.'

'Then why are you so sad?' Kiana asked, suddenly feeling like a lost child before Asal's sorrowful beauty.

'I know she is in love with me, but she's lying to me about her sex life . . . I feel she's sleeping with other people – some of them might even be in this room.' Asal looked around, her almond-shaped eyes round and wide, her dark pupils scanning the room.

Kiana felt deeply sorry for her, this was madness in its purest form. 'Sorry to say this, but you are ruining something really special and beautiful with these unreasonable feelings, for which you have no evidence!' Kiana stared directly into Asal's eyes, suddenly feeling strong; this was her chance to rescue her and her cousin, to rescue love, and defeat madness. 'Nobody knows Sayeh better than I do. She's just charming, and she likes being noticed by people. But she's not a liar. I swear on my mother's life Sayeh wouldn't cheat on you. She would've told me if she had. Why would she? Look at you, you're her dream. She fought with the whole family to be with you. I witnessed that, and I fought for you guys too.'

Asal seemed pensive for a moment, chin in hand, nodding her head, then she said, 'Thank you for saying these words to me. Most of my friends wouldn't for some reason. I think you might be right, I've been experiencing a terrible fear of loss since I lost my mother two years ago. Perhaps it's that. You are absolutely right, *azizam*, I should trust her more, because I am also well aware that she worships me.'

Kiana was pleased she had a good opportunity to save this love. 'And you are so clever! You've diagnosed your issue. My cousin isn't a liar. And she's definitely not a cheater!'

Asal embraced Kiana tight, saying, 'Thank you! The crystal rose is so elegant, but this was the real birthday present you gave me, Kiana.' Kiana held onto her, and they danced together for about ten minutes, until Asal was surrounded with some of her other friends, clapping and chanting, '*Tavalodet Mobarak!*'

Kiana was dancing to *Billie Jean*, feeling elated when the beautiful long-haired boy approached her and wordlessly danced with her. Now this party was the best she'd been to in a while. Kiana didn't remember the last time she felt so alive. She wanted to kiss him but was too shy. She decided to give it time; it wasn't even midnight yet.

At eleven thirty, the long-haired boy declared that he had to go and find his 'lost boyfriend'; 'he's really bad with directions! But the size of his dick makes up for that, we'll be back soon; I'd like you to meet him!'

Kiana forced a smile and said she'd love to meet 'the amazing dick' too. The long-haired boy laughed so loudly that

Sayeh joined them saying, 'Isn't she the funniest?' and kissed Kiana's cheeks. Kiana could smell her father's red wine on her breath, excused herself and went to the bathroom.

After washing her hands, she looked in the enormous mirror. What was wrong with her? Why couldn't she cure her loneliness? Why couldn't she have what her cousin had? She stared hard into the mirror. She definitely wasn't ugly, although she knew she wasn't as eye-catching as her cousin or Asal. But she wasn't bad to look at, some people even assumed she and Sayeh were sisters. Although they couldn't believe that Sayeh was two years older than her. But unlike Sayeh and Asal, Kiana was terrified of putting on make-up, apart from a greasy layer of her mother's old pink lipstick on special occasions. Why couldn't she find a funky lipstick to paint her lips with like Asal and Sayeh? And find movie-style romance, intense and a bit mad, but real, passionate, sexy, and eternal? Perhaps she could start being more out there tonight, in this incredible party full of beautiful interesting people and the possibility of love.

Kiana noticed the mirror was actually the door of a cupboard; she opened it to find it brimming with make-up products, some of them too old and broken to even touch. She also found two blue lipsticks: one was broken and the other, almost empty. How could anyone run out of a blue lipstick? She also found a stash of black eyeliners, different brands that she hadn't heard of. She recognised the brand her mother had years ago, BELL. A small, golden one. This probably belonged to her aunt, Sayeh's mother. There were also other brands, including one called Master Drama by Maybelline, two by MAC, Smoulder and Feline – she wasn't sure what 'Feline' meant. And there were five more by a brand that Kiana hadn't heard of before: Urban Decay. It was probably Sayeh's new favourite brand that her sister had been ordered to bring back from Italy. One of the Urban Decay eyeliners seemed brand new. Kiana took it and looked at it closely. It was called *Perversion*. Kiana felt naughty as she pulled the cap, and pulled down her lower lid like she'd seen Sayeh doing it, and lined her waterline. The eyeliner was extremely black and creamy. Already she looked much sexier. She could easily be related to that long-haired boy and be sisters with Sayeh. She was going to put some on her left eye too, when she heard a scream.

It didn't sound like a scream of joy, but a roar. The roar of a wounded animal. Kiana froze, not sure what to do. She put the eyeliner back in the mirrored cupboard before leaving the bathroom. Her heart was thumping so hard that her pleasant intoxication vanished and was replaced with anxiety. The source of the scream was the only bedroom, adjacent to the bathroom. Kiana opened the door without knocking to find Asal screaming and weeping, her blue lipstick bleeding into her chin. Sayeh was standing beside her, saying, 'Please, please, not in front of people,' trying to touch Asal's waist. Asal pushed her hand away, shouting, 'well, you've fucked half of them!'

Two other people, a man and a woman were standing on the other side of the room, looking terrified.

'Fuck off!' Asal screamed at them.

The woman went pale and whispered, 'Can I have my phone back?'

Asal threw a smart phone in her direction which landed on the floor. The woman pounced on her phone, and left the room in a second, with the man following her.

Kiana wasn't sure what to make of the situation. She knew she was suddenly noticed by Asal who yelled at her, 'Who knew you'd be a liar too, just like your cousin? Why did you have to cover up for her?'

'I . . . I . . .' Kiana stammered, 'What?' She noticed there was also another phone in Asal's hand. And she recognised her cousin's iPhone 6 with the blood red leather cover.

'Please give me back my phone,' Sayeh implored.

Asal jumped away from her and started reading from the phone, '*I've never kissed a woman before, but your kiss made me want to!* Random stranger from Tinder. Ew!' Asal's voice quivered.

Sayeh stepped closer to her, 'please return my phone,'

Asal pushed her away, 'If you come any closer, I will beat you to death. Do not touch me,' she continued reading from the phone, '*I want to be sucked and fucked by you again.* Tara, one of our so-called mutual friends who is now dancing in our living room with her boyfriend . . . also, fuck your taste!'

Despite her initial confusion and denial, Kiana was starting to see what was happening. She shot a desperate glance at Sayeh, but Sayeh was weeping and saying to Asal, 'Please stop! People are going to notice.'

'I don't care,' Asal said, reading from the phone again, '*I want to kiss you again* . . . This is from Leila! She's also dancing in the living room, *my* living room!' Asal's voice was getting louder, as Sayeh was begging her to stop by repeating, 'People are going to hear.'

Asal stopped reading the phone, and looking directly at Sayeh, she said, 'Don't worry, people are too drunk and the music is too loud for them to notice what a lying whore you are. As for those treacherous sluts, I'll deal with them later.'

Then she turned her head towards Kiana, who was trans-fixed. 'Did you know? She tells you everything! Did you also lie to me? To cover up for your nasty cousin? What is wrong with you guys?'

Kiana felt she was suffocating and didn't know how to respond. Asal didn't wait for her response anyway, as she fell to the ground, banging Sayeh's phone onto the carpeted floor in stabbing movements. Sayeh was weeping, but she looked at Kiana and said, 'Could you please ask people to leave?'

Kiana stormed out of the bedroom, turned off the stereo and told the remaining guests one by one to leave. The long-haired boy giggled, saying, 'I bet now that they're drunk, they're getting some action, so they don't need us anymore! I think you should join them, *hunny* and have a *treesome.*'

Kiana wanted to punch him, but managed to say, 'they just want to sleep as they had too much to drink.'

After everyone left, Kiana went back to the bedroom, knocked on the door, and a broken voice commanded, 'come in.' She wasn't sure whose voice, Asal's or her cousin's. Asal was lying on the bed, facing the wall, eyes closed, the zip at the back of her dress was undone, and Sayeh was holding her from behind. Both their necks seemed a bit bruised. Sayeh turned in bed to face Kiana then asked, 'What happened to your face?'

'What?' Kiana said, noticing a long scratch on her cousin's cheekbone.

'You have eyeliner on just one eye.'

'I'm leaving, I got a cab.'

'It's dangerous at this hour, can't you stay on the sofa like you said you would?' Sayeh asked, matter-of-factly, still holding on to Asal, even though her head was turned towards Kiana.

'No, my Snapp is arriving.' Kiana realised it was the first time in her life she was rejecting a request from her cousin.

'Snapp at this hour is not to be trusted.'

'Shut the fuck up!' Kiana blurted, and her eyes filled with tears.

'I'm sorry,' Sayeh said, her silver eye shadow barely there. Kiana noticed without eye make-up, her cousin's eyes were neither large nor beautiful.

Kiana's mobile beeped.

'At least text me when you're home so I know you're safe.'

Kiana left without responding, shutting the bedroom door and the main door quietly behind herself.

Outside the flat, the air was cool and still. She found her cab, and wound down the window as soon as she sat in the backseat. To her relief, the driver wasn't interested in small talk either. Kiana stared at the obsidian sky, swallowing her tears. She'd never seen Tehran so dark and empty. All the way home, she felt she was going to vomit or weep in the cab.

She arrived home at three in the morning. The house was dark and quiet. She tiptoed to her bedroom, and threw herself on her bed, shoving her face onto her cold pillow, stifling a scream.

God's Mistake

S etareh noticed her journal lying seductively under her bed as she was leaving at half past seven to attend her eight o' clock lecture. She hesitated for a moment, wondering whether or not to hide her journal in its safe drawer, away from the prying eyes of her mother. But since she was late, she concluded her mother would probably leave the house shortly afterwards in order to go to work.

I even love the day after having sex. My hair smells like the cigarettes we smoked, my body is still sensitive. I'm alone in my single bed and I relish it. The memories of lust are keeping me ecstatic . . . when will it happen again? And with whom?

As she had worriedly predicted, she was half an hour late for her class: English Poetry 2. The lecturer was going to teach Byron's *When We Two Parted*. Setareh loved the poem, because it made her weep, thinking of her sister who had left the country four months ago.

Setareh knocked on the door uncomfortably, and the lecturer beckoned her to enter the classroom. Setareh sat on the nearest empty chair. The lecturer had already read the poem aloud and now the students were discussing the immorality of Lord Byron. Setareh loved Byron, because she identified with him, but she didn't feel like defending him, as she already felt like the anti-Christ for being late. And the class turned its attention to dramatic monologue anyway.

Today, I realised my two favourite poets were also atheists: Shelley and Byron. Shelley even has a book called The Necessity of Atheism, which I'd like to read, but where can I find it? Sima said she'd send it for me once she's in Australia – on the condition that I wouldn't be 'dramatic' when she's leaving. She says I'm giving her a guilty conscience. But the non-existent god knows I've tried to conceal my despair. The problem is, I simply can't imagine myself without her. Sometimes, I feel she's my real mother!! At least I don't have to lie to her about everything. She knows I've become an atheist and she's fine with it. She says she's agnostic – because science hasn't really disproved the existence of god yet, and there are so many mysteries in the world. For me, it's not even about science and its progression anymore. It's about how I can't stand religion, and how I can see it's capable of ruining the brightest people – like my mother – and the greatest countries – like well, why would I name it, you know which country I'm talking about! And now my sister is leaving me, because this fucking country is too suffocating.

After the class, Setareh left her chair and approached her best friend, who was sitting in the front row. Setareh winked at her, 'Have you decided what to wear yet?'

Mahsa avoided Setareh's eyes, her voice trembling. 'I need to talk to you.'

'What's wrong, honey?' Setareh asked, alarmed. Mahsa

was usually cheerful. Setareh considered her a true hedonist, and that was why she had chosen her as her best friend.

'Let's go out for a fag,' Mahsa whispered. 'I can't breathe in here!'

They scurried out of the Humanities department and passed the many trees to get to their sanctuary, where they could smoke and kiss without being warned by the security guards.

Mahsa took out her pack of slim Esse and handed it to Setareh. Setareh took one and lit it with her purple lighter, then took another one and put it in Mahsa's mouth while lighting it with her own cigarette. They loved doing this.

I think I'm falling in love with smoking, for two reasons: 1. Because it soothes me whenever I'm nervous, which is 99% of the time. Too bad I always have to do it in secret. But perhaps that's part of its charm? Oh and 2. It makes me feel closer to Mahsa.

'Tell me!' Setareh looked at Mahsa's disturbed expression and touched her arm. She had never seen Mahsa so concerned.

'I had a bad dream last night,' Mahsa murmured, 'about tonight's gathering. It was such a vivid nightmare.'

'What?' Setareh smirked. 'Is that all, hon?'

'You know, in the nightmare, the police raided the house and the four of us got arrested. They were discussing the number of lashes we deserved.'

'What are you implying?'

'Cancel tonight!' Mahsa hissed.

'Oh, come on! Since when have you become superstitious? Cancelling such a fun night for a stupid nightmare! Nobody will arrest us! Have you been watching low–brow satellite channels with your parents again? It's not even a huge, loud party. It's just a small gathering: you, me, Amin and his *hot* colleague. I showed you his picture. You said he was gorgeous. Apparently, he fancies you, too.' Setareh realised she was delivering a dramatic monologue, though not as well as Robert Browning.

'I'll come with you if you're adamant. But please, let's not jump into it,' said Mahsa.

Setareh narrowed her large eyes, and continued her dramatic monologue in a dreamy tone, 'Imagine, you and me in our new boots, and Amin and his hot colleague in their sexy jeans. Instrumental jazz in the background, and we are drinking Amin's amazing homemade *sharab*. I'm sitting on Amin's lap and French kissing him, my fingers pressing his long neck, while you and his beautiful colleague are exchanging flirtatious glances; temptation, flirtation, intoxication, exhibition, and ultimately orgasm. And I have an inkling Amin and his beautiful colleague are like you and me ... a bit sexual with each other ... How can you say no to all that?'

'I can't,' Mahsa confessed. 'But I'm scared. I don't even care much about being lashed; I'm worried about my old parents having to go through the shame and hell. Where are you telling your mum you're going?'

'Just a gathering with my female friends in your house, as usual. But, why have you become so paranoid? We're not living in Marjane Satrapi's comics. Tehran is the most hedonistic city in the world. When was the last time you had sex?'

'Seven and a half months ago,' Mahsa murmured.

'Oh my god! That's why you're getting all these

nightmares! You need to fuck Amin's sexy colleague to feel good again; and we both need to watch them make out.'

'Doesn't he have a name?' Mahsa asked.

'Does it matter?'

They both screamed with laughter.

Mahsa and Setareh had to attend the same lecture at eleven. It was in the Religious Studies department, and a mullah was teaching the History of Islam. Mahsa and Setareh sat beside each other at the back of the class and took out their pencil cases and notebooks, as they knew they were going to write to each other the whole time, too excited to concentrate on the history of Islam.

The mullah was saying, 'before the advent of Islam, Arabs lived like animals, they buried alive every female newborn. Islam and the prophet taught them how to value women and treat them right.' His voice was dry, as if he were choking on his chalk.

One of the students interrupted the mullah's speech nervously, 'So stoning women who commit adultery is a way of treating them right?'

The mullah responded with a question, 'Would any other student like to answer our sister's question?'

A student raised his hand and replied, 'How else would you treat women who commit adultery? Islam doesn't stone innocent women.'

The mullah smiled faintly and was about to carry on with his speech, when the nervous student shot back, 'Why can't you just divorce them?' her voice vibrating.

Setareh felt for her, but was slightly apprehensive of discussing religion in public.

Mahsa wrote to Setareh, 'I hate people who argue with the mullahs about Islam. What's the point? Now his fucking sermon is going to take longer!'

Setareh wrote back, 'I know! And we need time to get ready for tonight!'

Mahsa drew a flower and Setareh drew a caricature of the student who'd defended stoning adulterous women. They both laughed quietly, while the whole class was lost in the dust of the voice of the mullah recounting the battle of Khaybar.

The nervous student was gazing down on her book, silently livid. Setareh considered going to her and praising her after the class, but they didn't have time for that.

Behzad is sort of getting clingy. I think he thinks I'm his 'girlfriend' or something. Why can't people differentiate between love and lust? Anyway, I sense his expiry date is fast approaching. There's this new boy I've been chatting with online, and I think we might have amazing chemistry. His name is Amin. He has the nose of Apollo. Of course, he's had a nose job. But who hasn't? Well, apart from me, Sima, and Mahsa.

Also, I've been grappling with some strange doubts recently; perhaps, I should've studied Persian Literature instead of English. Don't get me wrong, I love my major and worked my arse off to get to only the best uni to study English Literature, but but but recently I've been reading Forough Farrokhzad again and I find her sensual poetry much more relatable and exciting than bits of Paradise Lost that we're being taught now. Have I made a mistake? Or is it just Milton boring me to death? Anyway, these days, only reading Forough and being touched by Mahsa make me feel better.

At one o'clock, Setareh and Mahsa decided not to have lunch and go straight home to 'recharge their batteries' for the evening.

Setareh was driving her new car – a black Peugeot 206. She had recently managed to get her driver's license and dived gratefully into the never-ending traffic of the streets of Tehran. She was extremely cautious. Mahsa was sitting next to her, forgetting to fasten her seatbelt as usual. Setareh played Placebo, and then turned it off when Brian Molko sang in an accusatory tone: 'You are one of god's mistakes.'

They didn't talk, as Setareh had told Mahsa before that she could not speak while driving. Setareh usually gave a ride to Mahsa to Vanak Square, from where she could take a cab straight to her house. During these rides, Mahsa's hand was always resting possessively on Setareh's thigh, which Setareh both loved and feared. She adored her relationship with Mahsa, but she was worried that someday Mahsa would want more and limit her, cutting out other people.

As Setareh was driving down from the university to the main square, Mahsa informed her that another Peugeot 206 was following them. The Peugeot sped up and was now moving alongside Setareh's car. Four boys were waving and signalling them to stop so they could exchange numbers; their car exploding with Beyoncé shrieking that she was 'crazy in love'. Setareh frowned at them and managed to focus on her driving. She despised it when male drivers harassed her. She abhorred it so much she imagined crashing into their cars.

'They're cute, though!' Mahsa mumbled.

They all looked the same to Setareh. The four of them had gelled, short hair.

'They're a bunch of losers!' Setareh pulled down her window and shouted at them, 'bugger off or I'll call the police!'

They booed her but left eventually.

When they arrived at Vanak Square, Mahsa thanked Setareh and slowly kissed her cheeks before getting out of the car.

'I'll come pick you up at six.' Setareh said.

'Are you sure? I can call a cab.'

'No, it's okay. Your house is on the way anyway. See you, *azizam*.'

Today I turned twenty. This was, of course, my saddest birthday as it's been two months and eleven days since Sima left. When people tell me I'll get used to it, I just want to smash their empty brains. One thing's for sure: it's not getting any easier. At times, I feel numb. I can only forget about her when I have sex. Too bad, I find most people deeply unappealing. Also, it's getting harder and harder to come up with new excuses to leave the house and spend an evening with a lover. Anyway, that's not really my problem now. My poor parents did their best so I'd have a nice birthday tonight. They took me to my favourite restaurant – this new, posh Japanese restaurant called Kenzo. We got stuck in traffic for three hours, but it was worth it. Mum paid the bill. And Dad gave me a pair of heart-shaped earrings made of purple stones. Then he said, 'I looked everywhere to find something purple for you!' I had no idea he knew purple is my favourite colour. We don't really converse that much. And yet he knew. I was tearful, and I told them it was because Sima is not here. But in actual fact, the tears were for Dad. Whenever he does something like this, I feel so much sadness and happiness at the same time that it's overwhelming.

He's so old, his hair is all white and thin. Please, don't get me wrong, I love Mum, too, I just sometimes find it unbearable to live with her. I aspire to someday become like her (minus the funny religion, of course). It's not the same with Dad. Sometimes, we're just watching TV, and I'm incredibly happy to be in his presence, whereas I feel the opposite about Mum. She works so hard for this family (as she keeps reminding us!) and I appreciate that, but I just feel uncomfortable around her. Perhaps because she talks so much, so intensely all the time and asks too many questions, while Dad is usually taciturn. Or perhaps simply because he's a better person: he's noble and decent. But, unfortunately, I'm nothing like him; I am a total bastard. Sima is like my Dad. But let's not talk about Sima. These are supposed to be the pages of pleasure, not pain. Seeing Mahsa tomorrow; her family are away and we'll have the whole house to ourselves – to study of course! Hahaha. I know we will get drunk and give each other like five orgasms again, I am counting the seconds. (Would it be embarrassing if I ask her to read me some early Forough too?)

When Setareh arrived home, exhausted and starving, she found out her mother was home. Her mother would usually get back from work at three o'clock. Now it was about two. Setareh smiled at her and said hello, but her mother glared at her instead of greeting her like usual. Setareh noticed her mother's eyes were bloodshot. 'What's wrong, Mum? Are you all right?'

Her mother looked away and set her jaw. Setareh was afraid, 'Is Dad all right?' Do you have any news from Sima?'

'Yes, everyone is all right, but you,' her mother screamed. 'You sick whore!'

Now Setareh was more confused rather than scared. Her

mother threw a tantrum every now and then, but this was the first time she called Setareh a 'whore'. Setareh didn't know her mother even knew that word.

'Why are you back so soon?' Setareh asked her.

'I didn't go to work today. We had a cleaner. I asked him to leave, though,' her mother burst into hysterical tears. 'I wish I'd died and hadn't seen how my child has turned out!'

Setareh took off her *manteau* and black scarf. 'Mum, have you gone mad?' she tried to sound cool, but her voice was trembling. She headed to her room to escape. As soon as she stepped in, she realised what was wrong with her mother. Her room was clearly tidier, and her journal wasn't under her bed anymore, but was violated, bleeding on the floor in the middle of her room: purple and vulnerable, hot like a loaded gun, triggered by an invisible hand – the hand of God.

I feel like Humbert Humbert at the beginning of Lolita, where he acknowledges that it is 'madness' to keep a diary, but he just has to do it because of 'a strange thrill'. Well, at least, I don't fancy underage people! No, I don't think I'm a 'bad' person. Perhaps, I am a bit too much into hedonism. But what's the point of a perfect godless life – if not pleasure?

Setareh did not dare to leave her room; her appetite had just disappeared. Instead, her instinctive reaction was to lock the door and dive into the sofa near her bed, hoping to faint so she wouldn't be aware of what would happen next. Her mother was behind the door, grabbing the handle, pulling it up and down swiftly and then beating on it with her fists, 'Open the goddamned door! We need to talk! I want to tell you something!'

Setareh was trembling so violently she could not move the bolt.

'I said open the door! Or I'll call your dad and tell him what a lying slut his beloved daughter is!'

Setareh thought her mother might've been bluffing, but she was in no position to take any risks. She took a deep breath, leaned her forehead against the door, unlocked it, and let her hysterical mother in.

'I'll explain everything!' Setareh pleaded with her.

'Explain what? You're a disgrace! You've been fooling me! What's wrong with you? What did I do to deserve a daughter like this? We provided everything for you, and is that how you repay us, by lying to our face? By having the nastiest sort of secret life!'

'Mum, I'll explain. It's not what you think,' Setareh wondered miserably how to 'explain'. The explanations were all in the journal, which her mother had read. There was no other explanation. Everything was as clear as the sunny sky outside her window. And then it occurred to her to use Humbert's excuse. 'Mother, you know how I enjoy writing? You've always encouraged my writing.'

'What are you trying to say?'

'What you read is not my life. It's a story I've been writing. It's a novel about this woman with sexual complexes. You know I'm not really into that stuff myself.' Setareh said, widening her eyes, and slightly pouting her lips in an effort to look innocent and remorseful.

Her mother sighed loudly. Setareh felt her mother had turned into a rabid animal that was ready to slay her. 'You expect me to believe this bullshit? You think I'm stupid! I teach people your age at the university! I have a PhD for

God's sake! With your disgusting narcissism, no wonder you think that everybody is dumb but you!'

Setareh took a deep breath. 'Mother, I swear to God, what you read has no basis in reality, it's all my sick imagination.'

'What about the dates? The night you told us you were going to an Iftar ceremony in your university, you were going to that man's house or were doing stuff with another girl . . .' her mother trembled and screamed, 'Who is Amin?' and before Setareh got a chance to respond, her mother shouted even louder, 'I thought Mahsa was just a normal friend!'

Today I did something rather clever; I told Mum I was going to an Iftar ceremony in our university, when in actual fact I was going to Amin's flat with Mahsa. Amin was wearing a skirt and Mahsa put make-up on his face. He became so beautiful that I couldn't stop kissing him. Perhaps Ramadan is not that bad after all. I mean, this time it's worked to my advantage!

Setareh was speechless. Her nightmare finally came true: her dear religious mother had read her sinful journal. Setareh was ashamed and hurt, her mother was now weeping horribly loudly. Suddenly she stopped to attack Setareh again, 'And don't swear to God when you don't believe in him. I know you're a filthy atheist! This is all your father's fault for spoiling you so much! For letting you get away with everything! I couldn't raise you the way I wanted to!'

Setareh could not take this; she hated it when her mother blamed her father every time she was mad. 'Now I bet he'll be proud of you!'

Setareh found herself tearful. 'Mum, promise not to involve him. I'll do whatever you ask me to. He's old and fragile. Please don't punish him for my mistakes.'

Today something quite awkward happened. I was writing in you when Mum suddenly opened my door under the pretext of bringing me tea. I quickly closed you and acted as though I'd been staring out of the window, but I'm almost sure she knew I was writing. She didn't mention it, though, just banged the damned cup of tea on my desk, and sat on my bed, asking me about my day.

Setareh looked at the clock on her wall. It was half past four. Her father would usually get home around seven. And her mother exclaimed again, 'You're a liar! You don't even like your major! After fighting with all of us to study such a useless major! Even your father wasn't on board. He wanted you to become a lawyer,' upon hearing these words, Setareh's tears streamed down her face, her mother didn't stop, 'and now you don't even want it anymore! You want to shift to an even more useless major! So you'll have a good excuse to read that whore's poetry the whole time!'

Setareh did not know how to respond. She felt something was growing in her throat, suffocating her. Her tears dried; her head was imploding. This was a horrible attack, even for her mother. For a fleeting moment, Setareh wished they had both been dead.

Her mother's gaze was now dangerously quiet. Setareh could not look back at her, so she stared at the wooden-framed clock ticking, a time bomb.

Her mother finally got up, muttering 'I need to do my afternoon prayers, it's getting dark.' Setareh was relieved her mother was leaving. She crawled to the kitchen as her stomach was rumbling, found some *Sangak* bread and Tabriz cheese, and swallowed them almost without chewing, which made her nauseated. She wanted to vanish.

Then it occurred to her that Mahsa was probably getting ready now. Setareh texted her and Amin and cancelled. Mahsa immediately texted back: plz B safe. LuV U :*. And Setareh was sure she loved Mahsa too and wished she would be kissing her lips instead of trying to survive her mother's rage, but didn't dare texting back, in case her mother would proceed to confiscate her phone.

While Setareh was making tea, her mother crept into the kitchen. She had not taken off her floral chador after her *namaz. This is a statement.* Setareh shuddered as she thought it.

'Sleeping around and blasphemy aren't the whole problem. The main problem is how you've been fooling us for two years . . . I wonder what else you're capable of. A person who lies like this to her parents . . .'

Setareh sighed, and poured tea from the floral china tea pot. 'You want tea?' she asked under her breath.

'No, I want death!' her mother yelled. 'Oh God!'

'You made me lie,' Setareh heard herself saying.

'What!'

'If you weren't so narrow-minded and *ommol*, I would've told you everything . . . even though it's really my private life and none of your business!' her words burned her tongue more than the tea.

'What nonsense! Private life! Nobody has a private life here! We all live under the same roof! And we should obey the same rules. It's true that your dad and I aren't strictly religious, but we still respect some things. And we respect ourselves. We don't like sluts and liars!'

'Speak for yourself. My dad is different from you. He's not even religious.'

'I know! That's why it's his fault that you're like this. You used to be so innocent, and now look at you! Look at those dark circles under your eyes! The wrinkles around your mouth! And you're only nineteen! It's all the secret cigarettes you smoke and the alcohol you drink . . . and you probably have sexually transmitted diseases . . . I mean, you don't even have a proper boyfriend . . . you've been with several men and women!' Her mother wept again. 'I can't believe my daughter is an alcoholic!'

Setareh was dejected and furious. Furious at everything. At sex, at alcohol, at her mother, but mostly at herself for leaving her journal unguarded under her bed.

Her mother ran out of the kitchen, picked up the phone, and started dialling. Setareh ran after her, thinking her mother was going to contact her father. She tried to grab the phone, but her mother pushed her away.

Setareh found herself on the floor, weeping. 'Please, don't call dad. I'll do whatever you want me to. I'll change myself and become who you want me to be.'

Setareh wasn't as scared of her father as she had been of her mother; she was merely insanely worried about him. Also, she didn't want her gentle father to get dragged into her mother's terrifying drama. He was old and small, and he'd never shout back when her mother was accusing him of ruining everything. He would just grow older and smaller.

'I'm not phoning that useless man anyway. I'm calling

Sima to see what she thinks we should do with her *innocent* little sister!'

Setareh felt she was in a nightmare; she just stood there and watched her mother shaking with the black phone in her right hand, shouting to Sima, 'Your sister is ill! Can you take her abroad to cure her?

'No, I don't need to see the tests! It's just obvious! You haven't seen how she's been looking recently, although apparently she thinks she's Venus because people like to sleep with her!

'No, listen, Sima, of course I'm not a *Basiji*! I just hate liars and sinners! She's been lying to our face, hiding her sick life from us like a professional liar! I can't stand her in this house! I feel betrayed!' After shouting this, her mother became silent for a few seconds, then said, 'I can't believe you're taking her side.' Setareh was trying to guess what Sima was saying in response. Her mother reiterated, 'No, you are taking her side, because you pity her. But we should do something about her, get some help, instead of pitying her!'

Setareh couldn't take it anymore. She ran to her room, and shut the door behind her. She sheltered under her blue duvet and closed her eyes, wishing for an abrupt death. After a few seconds, she got up restlessly, took her guilty journal and tore every page, then threw the shreds of paper out of her window, letting the autumn wind take them far away.

'The thought of suicide is a great consolation: by means of it, one gets through many a dark night.' But I'm so sad that I'm actually considering suicide. Sima left the country last night. I haven't been able to stop my tears since she left. Mum and Dad are worried about me. I feel quite feverish, even though it's summer. Sima is

not just my sister, she's also my best friend, and let's face it, my mother! I don't know what I'm writing. I just know writing has always helped me deal with (digest?!) my problems. But this time I don't think anything can help me; no amount of writing or sex or alcohol or cigarettes will rescue me. They might soothe me. At the moment the only thing that distinguishes me from a corpse is an abject hatred. I never felt I could actually hate my country. I never hated it because of its religion, pollution, government and the usual stuff that people whine about day and night. But I hate it now – because it separated my sister from me. When will I see Sima again? I'm nineteen now, perhaps when I'm in my twenties. Oh god, oh fucking god.

When she turned away, she saw her mother was back in her room, pale in her greyish chador, like a ghost.

'I see you've also manipulated your sister!' her mother stated. 'She accused me of being a *Basiji* and repeated that nonsense you gave me earlier about your private life. Even so, she agreed that you're a liar!'

Setareh repeated herself, because she knew her mother was going to repeat herself for a long time. 'You made me lie, you prude.'

Her mother did not scream this time. 'I'm not a prude. If I were one of those illiterate mothers, I would've forced you to quit university and stay home, but I'm not.'

'Those illiterate mothers are more bearable – they're not as self-righteous and self-assured as you are, and actually not all of them are as *ommol* as you are!'

'I only want the best for my daughter,' her mother wept again. Setareh felt hopeless and hateful. They were arguing again.

'You're one of those immoral atheists ... at least your father believes in morality. You believe in NOTHING! Are you a *hamjensbaz*?' her mother was half-shouting again.

Neither of them was crying anymore. Then Setareh heard the sound of the key in the keyhole, and her father was in the house. 'Hello!'

He emerged in Setareh's room and glanced at them, 'Is everything okay?'

Setareh was tongue-tied, her heart beating so loudly she was sure her father could hear it, but to her utter relief her mother said in her convincing tone, 'Yes, we're just arguing. If you're hungry, there's food in the pot on the oven; *gheimeh* stew and rice.'

'Oh, thank you!'

Setareh forced a smile at her father and thought, no matter what, she was going to protect him for good: she decided that she would do anything to ensure he wouldn't get hurt. Her father embraced her. 'How's my beautiful daughter?'

'I'm okay, thanks, a bit knackered, though. Too many classes at uni today. How are you?' Setareh responded like a robot.

Her mother narrowed her eyes at her, and Setareh trembled. Her father let her go and said, while exiting her room, 'If you're tired, get some rest instead of arguing with your darling mother!' and disappeared in the kitchen.

When he left, her mother shut the door. Setareh said mournfully, 'thanks for not telling him,' her dark eyes glistening with tears.

'I decided not to. Not because of you, but because he's a weak, useless man and will worsen the situation with his inefficiency. He can only be a good father to his damned university. That's why he's obsessed with it.'

Setareh yearned to tell her mother to shut up, but she managed to somehow control her fury. She was going to lose this battle, regardless of whether she was right or wrong. Her mother would never lose. She was the most powerful person Setareh knew and she could easily imagine her mother shattering her and her father. Setareh decided to bargain, to lie again.

'Mum, you know what?'

'What?'

'I really want to apologise. I really regret the things I've done. You have no idea how much I hate myself for them. It's all Mahsa's fault. She's corrupted me. You remember, I've always been interested in reading, I'm still very indoorsy. I hate sex and drinking. I only smoke because I feel sorry for myself. I'm sorry I don't pray. I feel I am losing God. I feel God has abandoned me.' Setareh shed a tear and was praying to her non-existent god that her lies could fool her clever mother. She paused to look at her mother's expression. Her mother seemed ponderous and was surprisingly quiet. Setareh continued her dramatic monologue, 'You know I've been feeling so lonely since Sima left.'

'Yes, I read this in your journal,' her mother's coarse voice softened into a murmur, like ice in the heat. 'You two were very close. But she never behaved like you, she's a respectable engineer in Australia, engaged to a good Australian man. I always knew you two were different, but not this much ... also, so you know, God never forsakes his servants.'

'Mum, I'm sorry, I was only eighteen when I started

going crazy. It all happened after I met my university friends – whom I despise now. Mum! I will not talk to them anymore. I promise you. I'm your daughter, please believe me.' Setareh's voice was shaking so deeply she almost believed her own words for a moment, although she was uncertain whether or not her mother bought them. To her utter surprise and satisfaction, her mother looked up and said, 'Interesting that I always had a bad feeling about Mahsa ... I haven't forgiven you yet, but I'm willing to give you a second chance to see how you behave. We'll see, okay?' her voice was suddenly calm and forgiving.

Setareh almost fell to her knees, 'Thank you, mother! Thanks!' she thought she should probably quit sex, alcohol and Mahsa for at least six months. The peace was worth it though, she concluded.

Oshima

Nasim is lying on the comfortable bed her aunt has given her. To her relief, her parents have gone back to Iran. *The real holiday has just begun*, she thinks.

Her aunt is smoking in the kitchen. It seems to Nasim that smoking is the only thing she does. Nasim is tempted by the fumes of her cigarette, which seep under her duvet. Reading Haruki Murakami's *Kafka on the Shore*, she is smitten with one of the characters and cannot get enough of him. Having lost interest in the plot, she is now focusing solely on any trace of that one particular character: Oshima. His sweetness, androgyny and sophistication are extremely appealing to Nasim. She slips her right hand under her duvet, inside her warm pyjamas. Oshima is talking about Schubert; about how Schubert's apparent imperfection has made his music perfect. Nasim puts her book aside. She can still smell the lingering smoke of her aunt's cigarette. Afraid of making a sound, she stops touching herself.

Nasim takes off her pyjamas and puts on a pair of maroon skinny jeans with a black jumper, and sprays some perfume on her long neck – *Guilty* by Gucci. In the mirror, she observes how the drops of the perfume trickle down her neck. Then she throws on her coat in order not to catch a cold, puts on her black boots and saunters to the kitchen.

'You look gorgeous, darling!' her aunt informs her in her scratchy, coughing voice, her small eyes shining. 'Thank you, auntie,' Nasim kisses her on the cheek, 'You're cute!'

Cologne is glowing with rain. Nasim adores the rain, unlike most people who live in Cologne; they constantly complain about the rain. *Rain is terrible, it's just bad luck.* She's aware of their moaning and does not even try to be understanding. *Really, people? Is that your problem? Some drops of rain from heaven? Get a life. Get a fucking life, you fucking people.* She loves to insult people – in her head.

Nasim is studying German in the café. It is four in the afternoon; she allows herself to start drinking. She orders a beer. 'Germans have the worst history, and the best beer,' her aunt informs her every night, slurping her dark wine in the dim kitchen.

Nasim orders Kölsch. She tries to order in German. The waiter laughs. 'You are really improving.' His skin is pale, his cheekbones as sharp as the Milad Tower of Tehran, his eyes calmly blue, his mouth rosy and as small as a child's. His hair is blond and curly, and he is very tall. Nasim feels hot from his blinding beauty. He pours her beer in a 0.2 glass, while she stares at his dainty hands.

Nasim licks the head of the beer, saying, 'That's my favourite part.'

He stares at her. Nasim thinks he might be even younger than her: twenty maybe. His youth touches her as deeply as if she were an old, dying person. She feels like holding his hands while sucking his lips – violently.

'Is that your perfume?' Nasim says. *'Du riechst so gut!'*

The waiter looks at her amusingly, a bit taken aback. 'It is! I like your shoes,' and points at her knee-high boots.

'I bought them from Schildergasse. I fell in love with them the moment I saw them.' She lies in order to sound like the alluring women in mainstream movies. She could never fall in love with a pair of shoes. She bought them in a massive sale in Tehran, has carried them all the way to Cologne inside her half-empty suitcase – a baby's corpse in its miniscule coffin.

'Touch,' she puts her right foot on the chair, 'the quality of the leather is amazing!'

The waiter touches it swiftly, as if he were touching a bonfire.

'Now refill my glass, please. Why are the glasses so small?'

When she leaves the café after two hours of studying German language and German men, she sees the waiter standing outside the café, leaning against the wall, looking at the trees, oblivious of his own beauty.

On the way home, she realises she is drunk. Nasim loves being drunk on beer. It gives her such a peaceful intoxication. When she is inebriated she is full of life and love, and does not think about the news and the expiry date on her Schengen visa. She feels she has always lived in Germany. And yet, she has not found a university willing to accept her. As soon as they realise her German is poor, her English mediocre, and her bachelor's is from Iran, they ditch her, granting fake, polite smiles. Nasim hates these smiles. She feels like burning down every university that rejects her.

Nasim goes to the café on a regular basis. Sometimes, the beautiful waiter serves her and she ignores him as part of the game. But after a while, she can't. Instinct is clawing at her skin. Her skin craves his. At four o' clock one afternoon, when he is wordlessly refilling her glass with Kölsch, Nasim notices he is wearing blue nail varnish on three of his nails; she gives up. Gazing at his hands, she feels like licking his blue nails, but instead manages to say '*Wie gehts?*'

The waiter seems surprised at her broken silence. 'I'm good, thanks, and you?'

Nasim thinks his German accent is like pepper on English language. She likes pepper.

'I'm good, too, *danke*. What's your name? *Ich bin Nasim.*'

'I am Valentin.'

'A beautiful name for a beautiful boy!' Nasim stares into his eyes and smiles, which make him blush and look away. His coyness and innocence warm her up. 'Do you live alone, Valentin?'

'Yes. In a small flat near here.'

'I see. How many hours are you working today?'

'One more hour and then I'll go home.'

'Is it okay if I come with you?' Nasim gazes hard into his eyes.

Valentin is even more surprised. His white skin turns red, 'Why?'

'You'll see once we get there.'

*

122

Valentin's flat is tiny but neat. There's not much furniture around, just one double bed, a greyish green carpet and two green sofas in the small living room, which is adjoined to the open kitchen.

'*Sehr chic*, Valentin.'

'Thank you,' Valentin chuckles. 'Would you like something to eat or drink?'

Nasim takes his hands and pushes him towards the bed. 'No, you're enough.' Valentin lies on his back while Nasim takes off her clothes and then climbs on top of him, helping him to take off his black shirt and blue jeans.

His body is a fine sculpture, every line and curve in shape. It looks so right, so beautiful, so perfect. Nasim kisses his lips and goes down to his long, scented neck and hard nipples. He touches her breasts and smiles at her, 'You are beautiful.'

'Shhh. Either speak German or don't talk at all.'

For some reason Valentin chooses the second option. Nasim rides him as soon as he's hard and after a few minutes finds herself giving him a thunderous slap on the cheek, hoping he objects, so she can get into a naked physical fight with him. She would slap him even harder and scream, until someone bleeds and they stop the game – or not. But not only does he not object, but like Jesus Christ he offers his unslapped cheek to her. Nasim slaps Christ's other cheek even harder, observing how the seemingly bloodless skin is turning the colour of blood. She is almost choking with excitement. She chokes the boy till he barks like a puppy.

When she saunters back to her aunt's house, immensely satisfied, she thinks of finding a new café, considering it awkward to go to that same café after slapping and choking the waiter so hard.

Nasim sits in the bar that is close to her aunt's house, relishing the thought of being away from her mother and homeland for a while, hoping she can stay in Germany for good. Rainy Germany. *Rainy, sexy Germany.*

She spots a man sitting behind a corner table on the other side of the bar. His beauty is raw to her, not exactly sophisticated, but definitely eye-catching. She throws sideway glances at his hands, neck and hair. *He seems all right for a one-night stand,* Nasim concludes, nothing special but acceptable. Not exactly perfect, but hot enough. *I want to fuck you,* she almost declares under her breath. She sips her chamomile tea. He notices her and smiles at her. *Sexy thin lips. Those lips are made for sucking my pussy,* thinks Nasim. Suddenly she remembers the last time she had sex in Iran. It was last year, while her mother was at *Khatme An'aam,* reading the Quran with thirty other women, all nice and dressed-up, stuffing their stomachs with the delectable food of the hostess. Nasim even remembers the leftovers her mother brought home from that ceremony. It was the finest *fesenjan* stew Nasim ever had. She recalls the rich taste of cooked and crushed walnut in her mouth, and she was especially famished after the fierce sex she had had with her cousin. She devoured the stew and rice in a matter of seconds, while her mother kept saying, 'Eat some more, darling, this food has been blessed. Where is Donya? Did you guys study well? Did she leave? If she's still in your room, I'll take some blessed food for her as well . . .'

Nasim exclaimed without wanting to, spraying a few

brown drops of stew on her mother's face, 'Yes, she just had a shower! She'll join us in the kitchen in a second!'

Nasim does not smile, just stares hard at the man. He stares back. This could go on for a while. Nasim is imagining him in bed already, hoping he does not stink and smells nice. Like some cool cologne. Like the rainy weather of Cologne. She approaches him.

'*Hallo,*' she also wants to practice German.

The man responds to her in Farsi. '*Irani hasti?*'

Nasim chuckles in surprise.

'I can tell by your eyes,' he says. 'Only Persians have these eyes! We Iranians, we are an unfortunate nation, but not when it comes to looks!'

Nasim tries to go deaf and keeps imagining him, silenced, between the sheets.

Half an hour later they are walking down Domplatz, Nasim getting drawn to Kölner Dom, drowning in its beauty and symmetry. The man interrupts her pleasant drowning by grabbing her hands and exclaiming, 'Your hands are beautiful!'

'I like your hands, too,' she squeezes his back. 'Very well-shaped. *Man hand fetish am.* Your hands were the first thing I checked back in the café.'

'You are a what?' he asks.

'Nothing. I am a nothing.'

'What did you say you were doing here?' he enquires.

'I'm here on a Schengen visa, searching for universities, but no luck so far.'

'What do you want to study?'

'Psychology.'

'Psychologists are all crazy themselves!' he bursts into a laugh at his own remark.

Nasim does not laugh. Yet she tries to smile, and in a second she hates herself for trying to smile at his cheap joke just because she wants to fuck him. 'What are you doing here?' she asks.

'I'm a refugee. Was stuck in one of those nasty *Heims* for five years until my application got accepted two years ago. I'm an electrical technician.'

Nasim finds herself pitying him and wanting to sleep with him even more.

Nasim is in the man's tiny room, which smells of mouldy clothes and rotten lettuce. She does not know why she is there. While she is questioning herself in her head, the man is throwing his large tongue down her throat. Then gazes into her eyes, 'you're so *sexi*!'

'Tell me about your life in *Heim*. What was it like? I considered becoming a refugee for a while. But then I watched the YouTube videos and got terrified of the idea.'

'If you go there, you won't come out of it alive. It's a pigsty. A prison filled with uncivilised Africans and Arabs, and Nazi guardians who want us all dead, really. It stinks. If I had known about the conditions, I would've stayed in Iran.'

'Give me more details.'

'I don't want to talk about it, especially now.' the man takes off his shirt. Nasim finds herself taking off her jumper, too.

His technique in bed is poor. Nasim is bored. He does not perform cunnilingus. She wants to escape to her aunt's and read some more Murakami and masturbate over his characters. She wants to forget about the existence of *Heims* and Nazi guardians in Germany. He holds her tight after he comes, 'I'm not like the other men running away after fucking. I genuinely like you,' he says.

Nasim feels alarmed. She controls herself so as not to confess that she is 'like the other men', instead she twists out of his tight embrace, finding it difficult to breathe. Her instinctive reaction is to escape his clingy bed without wasting a word. But it is not easy.

'Do you like me, too?'

'Of course I do,' she says, avoiding his questioning eyes. 'That's why I'm here.'

'You don't act like you do,' he says, biting her index and middle fingers.

'What should I do? Chop off my fingers for you?' Nasim snaps, pulling out her hand out of his drooling mouth.

'Don't be disgusting! But . . .'

Nasim runs to the tiny bathroom, scrubs her hands with the cheap-looking German liquid soap, puts on her black jumper and trousers. 'I must go. My aunt is worried about me.'

She walks back to her aunt's house, thinking of enrolling in a German class, and head-banging in a German concert. Checking out boys, she thinks of getting some sex, some game. To her satisfaction, it is still raining. She wanders in the rain while wolfing down a *bratwurst*.

Nasim does not have a key to the house and is not sure how to ask for one without sounding too imposing and exploitative.

The aunt opens the door. The hall is half-dark as always.

Her aunt claims the light hurts her eyes. Nasim likes lights, she even likes lightning. Her aunt looks disturbed, 'Your mother called five times! Where were you?'

'I was reading in the café close by,' Nasim brings out a book out of her wet bag as evidence. It's a worn paperback of *Nausea*.

'Anyway, call her back,' says her aunt. 'She sounded really worried.'

'She always sounds worried,' Nasim states nervously. 'It's one of her weapons to control me.'

Her aunt laughs gladly, 'I like your wit, child. How's the uni–hunting going?'

'Not well, actually. Most of them require fluency in German.'

'You have plenty of time to learn German. You're only twenty, my dear!' her aunt says, lighting a cigarette, going towards the oven and flipping on the cooker fan.

'Twenty-two! And I don't have much time, considering the expiry date on my visa.'

'You're very young, sweetness, and obviously bright, too. I'm sure learning German would be like drinking water for you. Even though most immigrants complain that it's really difficult.' She puffs on her cigarette, 'by the way, there's a set of keys to the house on the cabinet for you. Make sure to take them before leaving the kitchen.'

'Oh, aunty! You didn't have to . . .'

'I had to, I'm not always awake or even here when you get back home. Nasim, darling, I want you to feel at home, okay?'

'I do! Even better than home. Home is suffocating. This is not.'

Nasim kisses her aunt's cheeks and goes back to her bed in her little room. She likes this room despite its size. It gives her the peace of mind she has been craving since her late teens.

She needs to take a shower to wash away the bad sex.

The hot water rains on her long body and she feels resurrected. For a while she does not do anything, then slowly starts by shampooing her straight, dark hair.

When she comes out of the shower, she sees the man's text on her mobile. 'I already miss you'. *What the actual fuck.* She smells obsessive behaviour. Nothing worries her more than when her lovers become obsessed with her, especially when they are not exactly Oshima. She remembers all the horrific news about obsessive lovers. 'Man throws acid on the girl's face who rejected his love' 'Jealous suitor stabs his love'.

Rubbing body lotion all over her damp body, Nasim tries to forget about the news and the man. Usually after her showers, when she lathers some coconut oil on her body, she feels so much love for herself, for her existence. For life. Life in Germany.

'Existence is an imperfection.' *But it must be pure perfection.* Sartre not only depresses her, but also bores her. Most existentialists do. She does not like to be depressed and bored. She closes *Nausea*, opens *Kafka on the Shore*.

Oshima is organising his sharp pencils. Murakami cannot stop describing him. Nasim is certain Murakami himself was insanely inspired when creating this character. She is interested to know the muse behind this creation. She craves to touch the inspiration behind this character, then chuckles at her silly, romantic idea. The man calls her; at first she ignores the call but cannot concentrate on Oshima anymore. She picks up.

'Why didn't you text me back? I got worried about you ... What are you doing?' his wording irritates her as much as his tone.

'I'm reading.'

'You read too much,' he informs her. 'That's why you're so weird!'

Nasim suddenly realises she cannot stand him. But she does not know how to ditch him without any fuss. She wishes for his utter disappearance without her having to spend energy.

'I gotta go. My aunt's calling me.'

'Go. Don't be mad at me. Did I yell?'

'No. Bye.' she can feel ice burning her tongue.

When she arrives home at ten from a long day of university hunting and studying German, her aunt is sleeping, and Nasim is grateful for that: she is not in the mood for talking to depressed old people right now. She feels old and depressed herself, whenever she remembers she has to return to Iran in a few weeks. Something tells her she will never get enrolled in a German college. *Fuck it. Let's enjoy life while I can.* She phones the Iranian man.

He sounds surprised to hear her voice.

'Let's fuck,' she commands.

'But it's eleven at night,' he responds, 'And I'm stuck with some friends.'

'Watching football?'

'Yeah, we are betting,' he says, 'I'm winning.'

'That's pathetic.'

'You are so cocky . . . do you wanna meet up tomorrow? To be honest, I'm dying to sleep with you again.'

'Yeah, tomorrow's fine,' she says, 'But before that can you describe our sex? Step by step.'

'Sorry, sexy, I don't want to get a hard-on in front of my mates, and the game's getting good.'

Nasim hears masculine shouts and hangs up in a sudden wave of nausea.

After brushing her teeth for twelve minutes, she gets into bed and falls into a deep sleep. She finds herself with her parents in a *Heim*; she can see the metal bars as vividly as she saw on YouTube, and then her mother's self-righteous moan, 'Happy now?' Nasim's torso twitches and she wakes. It's almost four minutes after midnight. Her eyes are stinging. She catches her breath, and tries to fall asleep again while thinking of beautiful things – like sex and Oshima. She finds herself in a vacant space with the beautiful waiter. They're talking about the quality of beer in Germany and Nasim stares at his hands, but his hands are too vague and he suddenly turns into Oshima. His tall body shortens and his curly blond hair turns into straight, black hair and his blue eyes turn into slanted, dark eyes, his cheekbones become even more sculpted, and instead of a bottle of beer, he gives his sharp pencils to Nasim. Nasim refuses, saying 'That's sweet of you, but I'm terrified of sharp objects.'

The following day after waking up from her vivid dreams with a crooked smile on her face, the first thing Nasim does is open Murakami's novel. She is about to finish it, but she does not want to. She cannot afford being without Oshima – *a perfect human being, amongst all the other imperfect creatures.*

Her mobile beeps. It is the man, asking what time to meet up. She feels dizzy and does not reply to his text. He calls her.

'How is my darling girl?'

'Terrible,' Nasim says, 'I have a terrible hangover.'

'Is that an excuse not to see me today?'

'I was just telling you how I feel – since you asked.'

'I did. But I did not expect that. I thought you'd be excited about being with me today?' he growls.

'I don't think excited is the right word . . .' she responds.

'It is. You were seducing me last night over the phone,' the man exclaims, 'You wanted me so bad!'

'Did I? The things we do when we are drunk!' Nasim laughs hysterically, yearning to choke on her laughter. 'Besides, last night is last night. The moment's gone, I'm afraid. Today I feel anything but horny. I'd like to finish this novel I'm reading.'

'What? You're cancelling on me?' he yells.

'I think I just did. Sorry.'

'Sorry my ass, you little cunt! To be honest with you, I'm quite disgusted with you and your behaviour. You're just a fuck, nothin' more than that.'

Nasim is shocked, but struggles to hold on, 'I'm afraid you're not even that.'

The man roars, 'Shut up, dirty whore. I knew you were worthless, since no sane girl gives in on the first date. You're a worthless whore! Has anyone ever told you that?'

'According to your retarded logic, you are a worthless whore, too. So you'd better just shut the fuck up and leave me alone.' Nasim is pleased with her own response, but does not know why her voice is shaking.

'You're going to pay for what you just said to me. I'm an honourable man and I can't stand being treated like that, especially by whores.'

'Fuck off, you stupid scumbag.' She hangs up on him quickly, so as not to hear his next response.

Even before getting into a fight with him, Nasim knew this man was not exactly Oshima, but she did not expect this degree of vulgarity either. The man's swear words keep piercing her ears like a thousand blazing needles, making her feel threatened. *What does he mean by I'm going to pay for what I said to him?* The news reports start circulating in her head like a monstrous hurricane, especially the most recent one, 'Rejected suitor stabs girl fifty-two times'.

They were both students, studying Persian Literature in a prestigious university in Tehran. They were both the same age as Nasim. The tragedy took place on a famous crowded bridge, *Modiriat,* about two o' clock in the afternoon, on the day of their graduation. The boy attacked the girl with a knife and did not stop. Nasim feels as if she heard the girl's screams.

The bridge was filled with a crowd, filming the exciting incident with their mobiles. People called the police, but the police arrived thirty minutes after the slaughter of the girl.

Nasim knows she cannot reason with this man.

Trembling under her duvet, Nasim is disgusted with her own weakness. She wants to stay strong, but she has just lost it. She keeps imagining the man attacking her. She knows she is physically strong. Thanks to all her Karate lessons, she knows she can defend herself in case somebody attacks her. But what if the man attacks her with a knife, like that literature student? Prior to that piece of news, Nasim was always under the illusion that literature students were the least violent people on the planet. *They read poetry and weep over its beauty . . . Such a tender bunch!*

She rolls over in her dark bed, already feeling stab wounds when somebody knocks on her door. It is of course her aunt. Picking up the nearest book, Nasim pretends to be reading, while hiding her shaking body under the duvet.

'What are you up to, hon? Enjoying your book?'

'Oh yes, it's amazing!' Nasim responds, thinking nothing can ever be *amazing*.

'Good. Did you talk to your Mum?'

'No . . .'

'Why are you so pale, sweetie?' her aunt stares at Nasim with her knowing eyes.

'Pale? I don't know. Am I?' Nasim looks in the mirror and sees a scary mask.

'How is uni-hunting going? Any luck? I really hope you can stay, too . . . you know I'm very lonely. And even though I won't be bothering you, the fact that someone else is in this haunted house, is delightful.'

'I would love to stay here. But I don't think it's possible for me to get accepted in a German university. I need an admission letter from a university to be able to apply for a student visa. My Schengen visa lasts for only three months.'

'What if it expires? What then?'

'I don't know. I'll be an illegal resident. They'd put me in those horrifying asylums – their modern gas chambers. Honestly, I much prefer Iran to that.'

'Oh no! We don't want that. Don't worry about the future. Who knows what it will bring us.' She kisses Nasim's pale forehead.

'Auntie . . .You have no idea how much I appreciate you letting me stay here.'

'I have no other reason but my own selfishness,' her aunt guffaws sweetly as she walks out of the room, leaving Nasim alone with her doubts and fears like myriad snakes in her bed.

Seven hours later, Nasim notices she has been in bed all day long and has not gone out due to the fear of running into the man and being stabbed. Sorrowfully, she thinks even Cologne cannot heal her wounds. Her mind goes to Ameneh Bahrami, whose suitor threw acid on her face a few years ago. She went through surgery numerous times, but still lost her facial features and eyesight.

Nasim cannot take it anymore.

Her problem is that she doesn't exactly know what it is she cannot bear. As long as she remembers, she has been feeling furious yet unable to articulate why. She just knows she wants to bite the world out of rage and frustration, chew it and swallow it down then defecate it, so perhaps it would change for better.

To distract herself from her stinging thoughts, she decides to watch a film: *Das Leben der Anderen*. She knows she should not watch this film, she has seen it before and knows it is merely going to make her feel worse. But she cannot help it. She watches it on her laptop in her bed and does not cry. She clenches her fists and has no tears in her eyes.

The ending is sort of hopeful, though. Nasim shuts down

her laptop and remembers she avoided giving her address to the man and calms down. She makes a pact to herself not to ever have sex again. It is not worth it. Nasim decides her *ommol* mother is right after all, pre-marital sex is not only a sin, but a perilous curse. She opens her pocket Shamloo and reads her favourite lines over and over again:

There is no more space
Your heart is filled with sorrow
The gods of all your skies have fallen to the ground
Like an orphan child, you've been left alone
You laugh from fear and a frivolous pride prevents you
from weeping.

Nasim suddenly realises that what she really wants is to return to Iran, to do an MA in Persian Literature in a top university, move out of her parents' house and Tehran, move to a city beside the sea, and fall in love with a woman who understands Murakami.

Art Lessons

Sara kissed Tara's lips so hard they both fell to the floor. While on top of her, Sara's hands travelled all over Tara's breasts. Only then did Sara realise they were both in their university attire in the university corridors; despite her fear, she could not stop touching Tara's clothed body, until an enormous dog appeared, deafening her with its barking, attacking them, blood dripping from its teeth.

Sara jumped awake, her heart pounding hard inside her scarlet pyjama top. She squinted at the blinding screen of her mobile. It was half past seven in the morning, time to get ready for the class of her favourite lecturer – Dr Tara Ahmadi.

Sara brushed her teeth carefully, and tried to make her puffy eyes wide with the help of a sparkling eye shadow and mascara. While applying the make-up, she considered the possible reactions of the woman in charge of checking their outfits and student ID cards at the entrance of the university. Sara adored the university so much that the menacing presence of the woman – whom her friends called The Dog – did not bother her much. In fact, she'd smile at the woman, and the smile seemed to tame her a bit. Sara wore a tight black *manteau* with her usual black scarf. She wore her favourite blue jeans and a pair of black Converses.

When she entered the kitchen, her mother said, 'Good morning, my love!' while pouring tea from the familiar blue tea pot. 'What time is your class starting today?'

'Half past eight.'

Sara sat at the table in the kitchen, opposite her mother, eating feta cheese and fresh *Sangak* bread while drinking sugary black tea. Like every morning, she knew her dad was already gone.

'I can give you a ride.'

Her mother offered to drive her to the university every time she had a class in the morning. Sara always accepted. At first it made her feel guilty, but after a while she realised her mother enjoyed it.

As soon as they got into the car, her mother declared, 'I love driving in the morning – no traffic!'

'I hate doing anything in the morning.' Sara murmured, still exhausted from the nightmare she had about Tara. Sara wound down her window.

Her mother got her attention by one clichéd question: 'are you enjoying being a university student?'

'Oh, yes!' Sara said, although unwilling to discuss it in the morning. 'Uni is much better than school. It's like a new world.'

'And you get to see a few boys, too,' her mother said.

'That is probably the only downside,' Sara declared. 'The boys at our uni stink.'

'Well, give them cologne or something.'

Sara laughed, knowing her mother was joking, meaning

to cheer her up. Sara stared at the naked autumnal trees that had mesmerised her since she was a child. When people asked her why she loved Tehran so much, she told them because Tehran was wild and vibrant with all kinds of shops, from hippy art shops selling Faber Castell products and strange-looking drawing pads to ancient-looking bazars, smelling like fresh lime and fish, to glitzy malls selling L'Oreal, Reebok, and Hello Kitty stickers. But Sara knew she was just saying what everyone wanted to hear and had heard before. She never told anyone that she was in love with the sombre-looking trees. When her mother's car stopped in front of the entry arch of the university, Sara kissed her cheeks as always, saying goodbye. 'I'll get home at five,' she said so she wouldn't worry.

'Be careful with The Dog,' her mother said.

Sara pulled her black scarf almost down her high forehead, so her dark locks weren't visible any more. Then she put on a pair of enormous sunglasses to conceal her made-up eyes.

The Dog was in her white stall as always, checking female students' IDs and outfits. Sara smiled and flashed her student card. The Dog shook her head in affirmation and faintly smiled back. Sara felt bad that they were calling her The Dog. She was a human after all. A human stuck in the system like everyone else. A human stuck in a stall. Sara assumed other students never smiled at her, they'd only look at her with disdainful hostility, like her friends, Maral and Sahar.

As soon as Sara saw her favourite lecturer in the corridor, she forgot about analysing The Dog's mentality and sympathising with her, her heart thumping hard.

'Hello!' Dr Tara Ahmadi sauntered towards her.

The lecturer was also wearing a black scarf – the same as Sara and every other woman at the university, but her wine-coloured locks framed her heart-shaped face. Sara remembered the sensation of their kisses in her dreams and wished she could stop blushing like a 14-year-old virgin.

'I know you're in my class,' Dr Ahmadi said, smiling at Sara, narrowing her large green eyes. She was quite small – up to Sara's shoulders. Sara tried to guess her age, but she failed and it didn't matter. 'But I don't remember your name, I'm afraid.'

How tragic. 'I'm Sara ... Salem.' She disliked her surname: a rare one, meaning 'healthy'. She hated the irony; she usually felt sick. Well, at least their first names rhymed.

'Yes, Sara. I'll remember that. Well, see you in class!' Dr Ahmadi smiled again, unlike her other lecturers. She was also much younger and prettier, which was, Sara presumed, why her other classmates looked down on her.

Sara loathed herself for not using this unique opportunity to flirt with Tara. To tell her teasingly, 'Oh, I can't believe you don't remember my name!' or to just compliment her on her teaching, or at least to stare *properly* into her eyes.

Tara was so informal. Not like the other professors, calling students by their surnames in imperious tones. She even memorised some students' first names. How very romantic. How kind and sweet and breathtaking.

Sara stepped into the class. The room smelled of the morning breath of sleepy strangers and stale sweat. She opened the large window, preparing the room for Dr Ahmadi, about whom the other students were already bitching; the fact that it was early in the morning didn't make a difference to this beloved ritual.

'She thinks she's different or something because she's got ugly red hair and creepy green eyes,' one of her friends, Maral, was saying. Sara wanted to defend Dr Ahmadi, but she could not bring herself to talk about her, fearing an explosion might occur if she uttered her name.

She wanted to say, 'she actually *is* different. And her eyes are anything but creepy. They are a beautiful mystery.'

'Rodin is so old-fashioned anyway. I wonder why anyone would get so passionate when talking about him,' her other friend, Sahar, expressed her priceless opinion.

'She's quite fuckable, though, I've got to admit.' Sara heard one of her other friends whispering: Ali. Sara was disgusted, but she hoped she'd heard it all wrong.

However, when Dr Ahmadi finally stepped into the class, all the gossip turned into silent reverence. Tara didn't smile like she'd smiled at Sara, but asked them sternly to hand in their assignments. While Sara was giving her homework to her, their hands touched briefly. Sara was pleased – pleased with the smallest progress and victory.

The lecturer then had a general go at students who failed to hand in their work, without naming names. But after around five minutes, she proceeded to talk about Rodin, becoming more and more passionate with every slide she showed. It was an unwritten and unspoken rule that naked sculptures were seldom shown – despite being blurred. Sara couldn't see the projections anyway, as she was only staring at Tara's long fingers. For a moment she even closed her eyes, letting herself sway on the tender waves of her deep voice.

'Sara,' Dr Ahmadi was calling her. 'Do you know this one? And can you tell us a bit about its history, please.'

Sara looked at the blurred slide show and knew it was Rodin's *Gates of Hell* inspired by Lorenzo Ghiberti's *Gates of Paradise*. But for some reason she could not say any of this. Tara was staring at her, and Sara felt crushed by the heaviness of the scrutiny of the whole class directed at her blushing face. She got so embarrassed that she wanted to escape. But it seemed to Sara that Tara understood her pause, therefore didn't wait for her pathetic response, and resumed explaining the piece herself, while smiling at Sara as if to reassure her that it was okay. Her gaze seemed to suggest that she knew Sara knew the piece, and even if she didn't, it wouldn't have mattered. Sara smiled faintly and looked down, her body melting inside her black *manteau*.

When the class finally finished, Sara felt it hadn't even started yet.

Tara vanished in an instant, and Sara was left with her friends and classmates. And yet she could still see Dr Ahmadi's slender hands all over the classroom. Sara was ecstatic upon noticing that Tara was not wearing a wedding ring.

It was ten o'clock and her next class was going to start at half past one. She considered going to the library and research-ing Rodin, but she knew concentration was impossible now. She looked at her group of friends, they were laughing loudly at some joke about the Turks, which wasn't even funny. Sara wondered if her red-haired flame had Turkish roots. After all, she had pale skin and green eyes. But then again, her ethnicity didn't matter, just like her age and marital status. Nothing really mattered but her hands and the powerful spark in her eyes when she smiled.

Sara smoked a cigarette with her group of friends in their secret place behind the university. It was a deserted garden with broken walls and no view from inside the campus, thus no fear of getting caught. They usually sat on one of the walls and chain smoked while talking obsessively about sex and dates. Two other girls and two boys. Sara liked Maral, but was also slightly intimidated by her. She was extremely tall and loud. She had bad skin and bad teeth with freakishly long eyelashes and a mound of black hair. She always wore thick, winged eyeliner. Sara knew she drew it on in the toilet after passing The Dog. Sara admired her determination, but found putting on eye liner in the public toilet in the morning slightly sickening too.

Sahar was sweet, delicate and the least talkative of the group. She was Sara's favourite. Sara was careful not to show it. She resented the fact that Sahar sometimes acted like Maral's slave. Ali and Farzad were the only boys from their university and major who did not smell funny, although Ali was always complaining about something, and Sara found Farzad secretly aggressive. And yet she couldn't think of hanging with any other group at the university.

'You girls are lucky,' Ali started lecturing them as soon as they settled down in the secret passage. 'You can just sit there and men come after you. I think I'm losing my eyesight due to excessive masturbation.'

'Believe me, we're all in the same boat,' Maral said. 'In fact, now I'm technically blind myself. Who are you?'

They all roared with laughter.

Farzad caught Sara's eyes when they were all laughing.

'What about you? It shouldn't be difficult for *you* to find someone,' he looked her up and down.

Sara felt uncomfortable, but she was getting used to Farzad's crude flirtation.

'Oh, well,' she didn't know what to say. Pretending not to know what he meant would sound silly and acknowledging her beauty would sound arrogant. 'No, it's not true.'

'Explain.' Maral looked straight at her as she spoke, puffing on her Bahman cigarette. Sara tried not to look directly at the big pimple on her nose, and to restrain the cough induced by her cigarette fumes.

'Well, I rarely see anyone whom I find attractive,' Sara said.

'Have you ever been with anyone? Or are you a virgin? Or both?' Maral asked.

'If this is a game, we should all play. But so you know, I'm not a virgin. I don't believe in 'saving it for my husband'.' They all laughed again. Sara thought anything could make them laugh, even the movement of an ant.

'So who was the lucky guy?' Farzad stared into her eyes, his eyes black. Sara found herself irritated by his aggressive beauty.

'Well, there's been a few. It's not what you think.'

'Yes, because she's *lez*!' Maral shouted while bursting into a hysterical laugh. Sahar hissed her, then looked at Sara with worried eyes. 'Is it true?'

'No,' Sara replied, not lying. 'I wouldn't call myself a *lezbian*. I've been with a few boys so far, and some of them were amazing. But sometimes I fancy women, too. When that feeling happens with someone, I don't really care about their gender, or anything else. It just happens.'

'Well, you're only nineteen.' Ali commented, sounding patronising because he was two years older than all of them.

Farzad was being quiet. Sara felt she'd talked a lot again, without thinking. And yet, she wanted to talk more. They were like her. They weren't like virgin girls from her high school. They were artsy and mischievous: they even smoked weed. Sara felt she was in the right place – a feeling she rarely experienced.

'Okay, now, it's your turn, Ali.'

By this time, they were all done with smoking. They were now walking side by side outside the university, going to the nearest fast food restaurant.

'I'd rather fuck a hamburger right now,' Ali said.

'Ew ... gross.' Maral retorted.

The fast food restaurant, *Sooper Estar,* smelled like ten dead cows. Sara felt like vomiting on the plastic red chairs, but didn't say anything. Ali was already raving about the hamburgers. Sara tried to think of beautiful things, like the lecturer's eyes: two green seas flooding her tiny world.

Instead of Coke, Sara ordered orange juice, at the expense of being mocked by the group. She had the feeling that Tara was the kind of person who would drink orange juice instead of coke. And she heard Farzad talking about her:

'What do you guys think of this new lecturer? I don't like female lecturers in general: they're all so chippy!'

Sara stared at her French fries, waiting for Maral to shoot down her love. But Maral was too busy wolfing down her sausage sandwich. Instead, Ali kept the ball rolling, 'She's *sexi*, though.'

'What's so *sexi* about her?' Farzad asked.

'I don't know, man,' Ali was speaking with his mouth

full. Sara noticed bread turning into paste on his tongue, and looked away. 'I just know, tonight, when I get home, I want to jerk off with her on my mind,' he closed his eyes. 'Doggie, of course.'

'That's very imaginative,' Maral was finally done with the sausage sandwich. 'I noticed she actually has nice boobs. I wish I had big boobs like that, instead of these two hazel nuts.'

Sara felt hot, and not in a good way. She could feel her ears burning under her black scarf, wishing she could shout at her friends to shut up.

'So you're like Sara. You're obsessed with boobs and women.' Farzad looked at Sara with hostile sarcasm in his eyes.

'Ugh. I don't fancy that red-haired whore anyway!' Maral made a noise as if she were vomiting. Sara was aware that from now on all her friends would call her love 'the red-haired whore'. That's how they nicknamed The Dog and some of their smelly classmates too, including Onion Head and Camel Tooth. That was how Maral and Ali expressed their creativity. Sara really wanted to throw up her fries and orange juice.

'Actually, we should ask Sara,' Ali addressed her. 'Do you find her *sexi*?'

'I think she's a good teacher,' Sara managed to mumble. The fries were hurting her throat.

'Don't be so boring,' Ali moaned. 'Would you ... fuck her? Apparently, she knows your first name ...'

Sara had fantasised about fucking Tara since the moment she first saw her two weeks ago. But somehow the word *fucking* had never occurred to her in relation to her red-haired

146

dream. If by 'fucking' they meant penetration, she had envisioned thrusting her tongue and love-sick fingers inside Tara so many times that sometimes she thought she had already done it. And inside Sara's head, it was always Tara, not Dr Ahmadi, not Ahmadi, not the 'red-haired whore' or anything else. Tara, four letters, forever rhyming with Sara. Her friends were waiting for her answer, all gazing at her like a bunch of hungry jackals.

Sara looked at her mobile screen. 'We should get going. Our next class starts in half an hour.' She knew they had all the time in the world to torture her.

'She's being evasive,' Maral said. 'Nobody's going anywhere until you reply.'

Sara laughed nervously at the absurdity of it all. 'Well . . .'

'Well?' they wouldn't even let her confess.

'She's very attractive,' the words poured from her mouth before she could taste them, yet she managed not to use the crude and aggressive English word her friends were fond of using, '*sexi*'. Sara found it difficult to stop once she allowed herself to talk about Tara, 'of course she is beautiful, especially when she's showing her Rodin slides and she gets more and more passionate with every piece she teaches.'

'Ooh la la,' Maral exclaimed joyfully. 'You have a *kerush* on her!' 'Another popular English word Sara could never bring herself to use. Especially when Hafez had already expressed these feelings in her mother tongue thousands of years ago: 'I am intoxicated on the wine of love'.

'But honestly she looks *esteraight*,' Farzad said. 'She probably has a gorilla as her husband.'

Sara didn't retort with the fact that Tara wasn't wearing a

wedding ring, or the way she'd smiled at her in the morning. Her smiles didn't look so *esteraight* to her.

Two weeks later, in the secret garden Farzad confessed in front of the whole group that he was in love with Sara.

'I know you claim to be *lez* or something to look more artsy and unique, but I don't care. I want you,' he stated. 'There, I said it.' He pronounced the word 'artsy' as though it had been a nasty insult. And it was.

To Sara his confession felt like an attack. She threw her cigarette on the bumpy ground and kept stamping on it with her black Converse, staring at it, seeking refuge in the corpse of her cigarette.

Maral replied faster than her. 'Aw! Farzad! I wish I could hold you now.'

'Please, don't. I don't want us all to get expelled for a hug. This is a hidden place, but still,' Ali said in his usual I'm-two-years-older-so-I-know-better tone of voice.

Sahar was looking at Sara. Sara looked back at her. Then she looked at Farzad. 'Thanks, my dear.'

'Is that all?' Farzad asked. And Sara caught Maral looking at her impatiently.

'Well, at the moment . . . I prefer to focus on my studies.' Sara knew she sounded fake.

Farzad kept staring at her, 'I didn't ask you to marry me, the least you can do is kiss me now.'

'Kiss him, yes!' Maral exclaimed.

Sara wanted to run away. She wanted to shelter in Dr Ahmadi's sunny office, whose walls were adorned with the postcards of beautifully-carved sculptures. None of them naked, of course. Sara always imagined Tara's house was brimming with naked sculptures. She'd seen it in her dreams. And she had a plan to get there, to be invited to her place. To touch her in her house.

Farzad, Maral, and Ali were staring at her, waiting for her kiss or rejection. Sara was speechless.

Sahar rescued her. 'You people are out of your mind. Sara, please don't kiss him, that'd be extremely risky and we might all end up getting expelled, or worse.'

'She has a point.' Ali agreed.

'So maybe, we can go somewhere else?' Farzad grabbed her hand so tight her fingers hurt.

Sara slowly released her hand. 'Farzad, I'm sorry. I like you as a friend. I don't have feelings for you. But thanks.' And turned to Sahar for no conscious reason.

'You were right. She's a fucking narcissist!' Farzad addressed Maral.

Maral defended herself. 'I never really said . . .'

'Stop. You don't need to explain.' Sara suddenly found it all so vulgar. She left the garden, and to her utter surprise and delight, she realised Sahar had joined her. Sahar *chose* her.

'We need to quit smoking,' she told Sahar. Sahar agreed.

Three days later, when Sara was sitting on a bench in the university's yard, awaiting and yearning for Dr Ahmadi's class, Ali emerged in front of her and asked her to apologise to Farzad and Maral, so they could all hang out as a *'sexi'* friendship group.

Sara did not know what exactly she had to apologise for. Therefore, she did not.

She then saw Farzad and Maral entering the class,

completely ignoring her. She felt perfectly secure and liked it. She didn't mind letting go of their '*sexi* friendship group' and being ignored by them for the rest of her life. She had Sahar by her side. And Tara had just asked the whole class to learn to look at an artefact like Sara did. She felt the whole class was jealous of her and the whole world was hers. And yet, she wanted more.

After that victorious class, Sara stopped studying her text books. Instead, she painted seas and oceans. Red seas and green oceans. Naked trees making love to each other. She even painted the ultimate cliché: black scarves around pale faces, a much-loved formula that she knew someday would win her a lucrative award in the West. She imagined Dr Tara Ahmadi naked and painted her. Sara considered it her strongest and most sensuous piece, so she hid it away in her closet, afraid someone might steal it.

During the fourth week of the autumn term, after exchanging a few long glances with Dr Ahmadi, the universe seemed to align for them. They bumped into each other in the corridor when neither of them were surrounded by others; just like in her nightmarish dream. Sara stepped closer and closer to Dr Ahmadi. 'Hello!' she murmured, then stopped for her to stop too. Tara responded to her joyous hello with a celebratory smile and uttered her name excitedly, as if Sara were a long-lost relative of hers. 'How are you, my dear?' she asked.

'Well, thank you! I've been painting a lot because of your class. It's the best class.'

Dr Ahmadi held her gaze and gave the response Sara was aiming for. 'I'd love to see those paintings!'

'I would love to show them to you!' Sara exclaimed, not caring about her stupid blushing face anymore.

'Can you bring them to me on Saturday at twelve?'

Sara had her Persian literature class then, which she also quite liked, but she said 'Of course! I'll bring as many as I can!'

Saturday was three days away; Sara stayed awake on Friday night choosing three paintings for Tara's eyes; she didn't want to take too many as she was planning to ask for more office sessions. All three paintings she chose had cubist backgrounds with subtle portraits of sombre-looking people.

Sara lied to Sahar about why she had to skip her Persian literature class. Headache. Home. When Sahar was in the literature class, Sara sneaked towards Dr Ahmadi's office, her heart thumping hard.

Sara knocked on the office door with her trembling left hand, her right hand gripping her paintings. Dr Ahmadi murmured, 'Come in.' Sara stepped in and found Dr Ahmadi sitting on the chair behind her writing desk, her MacBook open in front of her, a stanchion between her and Sara. Sara opened her mouth to say hello, but she couldn't say anything, she felt muted by the heaviness of her emotions towards Dr Ahmadi. Dr Ahmadi stared at her and smiled. 'Sit down. You look tired.'

Sara sat on the chair near her desk, on the verge of apologising for her tired face. Dr Ahmadi said, 'show me your paintings.' Sara handed them to her over the desk. Dr Ahmadi looked at each one of them for so long that Sara almost got bored. Staring at Sara's paintings closely and from afar replaced her smile with a serious frown. Then she touched the dried surface of the paintings, whispering, 'nice acrylic'. Sara controlled herself so as not to lick the fingers that were caressing her paintings. Instead she exclaimed 'yes!' in order to grab her attention. It worked, Dr Ahmadi put the paintings aside, saying, 'Well done!' She stared at Sara with loving eyes. Sara gazed back and smiled with her whole being. 'Do you like them?'

'Of course!' Dr Ahmadi exclaimed. Sara wanted to hold her and kiss her hands.

A month before the end of the term, Sara had already gained Dr Ahmadi's mobile number – their secret undisclosed even to Sahar. Sara texted Tara at least once every two weeks, asking for private meetings in her office under the pretext of showing her new paintings. Tara said Sara could never create anything ugly or weak. Anything she created had the glow of gorgeousness, 'the skill and the beauty of the Old Masters combined with the chaos of the new, you have both technique and imagination.'

Sara hadn't told anyone about her sweet extra office hours with Dr Ahmadi. Instead, she played them over in her head again and again, each time finding more magic. Tara's admiration and compliments were turning into the definition of the university for her, the definition of life. They were food: honey and chocolate. They felt better than strawberry ice cream in summer and carrot cake and cinnamon tea in winter. They were like spring showers, drowning Sara while making her fall more and more for spring. And they were always divine, even when they came at the expense of other people being disparaged.

'Sara, I'm sorry to say this, but sometimes I really get

frustrated with your classmates. I know you're friends with some of them. They show absolutely no interest in the subject or have any background knowledge. I wonder how they got accepted in the first place. I mean, this is a prestigious university and you know how difficult the entrance exam is.'

Sara wanted to respond by saying she adored how unprofessional she was being. Instead she said, 'By doing well in Arabic, English, and Theology. How else do you think?'

'Oh right!' Dr Ahmadi gazed at Sara more intensely and laughed, as if Sara's point was terribly witty.

'And just for the record, I'm not friends with them,' Sara said.

'Well, I'm not surprised,' Dr Ahmadi said. 'You're different. Although this other boy who sits at the back of the class is quite a talent, too.'

Sara suddenly felt out of breath and remained quiet for a bit, then added calmly, 'Yes, if only he wasn't so obsessed with Kandinsky and could widen his view. And themes.'

'Oh, I didn't notice that. Is he?'

'Well, you haven't seen as many of his works as I have. He has a point, but he repeats himself so much – this is just my opinion ...' Sara made a pause to make her sabotage sound more effective, 'but his paintings are starting to look more and more like nice copies of Kandinsky's late works ... I'm sorry, but I'm allergic to copies ... maybe I'm too old-fashioned. Maybe I should just accept that originality is dead.'

'Well, it isn't and you're not old-fashioned,' said Dr Ahmadi, but she seemed pensive. 'I'm not as familiar with these students and their works as you are. Also, I get the feeling most of them don't like me. I wonder why.'

'Oh, I'm sure it's not that,' Sara said. 'They're just intimidated by you.'

'But why? I try to be nice.'

'You are perfectly nice,' Sara could not keep from looking directly into her eyes. 'It's because you're young and beautiful.'

Tara laughed. 'I'm neither of those things.' Her shrill laughter, ringing in Sara's ears was the most beautiful piece of music Sara had ever absorbed.

Sara had become aware that Dr Tara Ahmadi was just pushing her to see how far she'd go, and Sara was willing to show her that she was willing to slaughter all the boundaries.

'You know you are. Especially when you talk about Rodin, and your voice becomes as colourful as Farshchian's miniatures.'

This time, Dr Ahmadi didn't laugh, only stared at Sara, looking as expressionless as some of the sculptures on her wall. And Sara looked away, as she did not find the strength to hold her gaze. She felt powerless and insane, suddenly surprised by the intensity of her own words and the whole scenario, and yet she relished it too much to be able to stop. Sara had noticed with hurt pride that Tara Ahmadi seldom mentioned Iranian or non-western artists in her class. Perhaps Farshchian's miniatures were too tacky and common for her taste. But Sara knew part of the reason she had fallen for Tara was her resemblance to Farshchian's mesmerising women.

In order to kill the heavy silence, Sara asked Dr Ahmadi to show her some of her own paintings. 'I'm sure they'd be massively inspirational to me.' This time she managed to stare directly into her eyes.

'You're too kind,' Tara smiled at her. 'But I don't paint.'

Sara was shocked. 'Why not?'

'I'm not talented, like you.' Tara was penetrating Sara with her green gaze. 'I'm a critic, not an artist.'

Sara was in shock, and so much in love.

'I'm happy with my life, don't worry, sweetheart,' Tara said as someone knocked on her door. The doctor looked at her watch. 'Sorry, I need to meet another student. See you in class soon!' she winked at Sara.

The other student barged in. Sara's saliva turned bitter with irrational hatred of the student who had dared to interrupt their sacred session. But she consoled herself with the fact that while the other student was ugly, she had been called sweetheart and winked at.

Sara had lost count of these meetings, the last one she recalled was number five. She was aiming to invite Tara Ahmadi to her house in the seventh session, when the university was closing, before and during the Persian New Year in the beginning of spring. She was trying to count again in the corridor, clutching her victorious canvases when she bumped into Farzad.

'Look who's here!' Farzad blocked her way.

'Move.' Sara murmured.

'Where were you? So many paintings! You're probably the most prolific student in the history of the university!' Farzad said, and as usual Sara wasn't certain whether it was a compliment or an insult. Therefore, she tried to go with the former, 'And possibly the most talented!' How easy it was to believe in herself when Dr Tara Ahmadi believed in her.

'I bet you've painted them to impress that red-haired whore!' Farzad blurted.

Sara felt so furious her heart raced, 'Get out of my way, loser!'

'Do you think no one has noticed your secret rendez-vous? And the way you two flirt with each other in class in front of everyone? So shameless and unsubtle. Why don't you two get a room and put yourselves and everyone else at rest?'

'Fuck off!' Sara roared, trembling. She felt like assaulting Farzad with her canvases.

'So, if you're still trying so hard to seduce her in the uni-versity, that means you haven't gotten into her pants yet?'

Sara pushed Farzad away. 'Stay away from me. Or I'll tell the authorities you've been harassing me.'

'Are you threatening me?'

Sara could smell the cheap marijuana on his breath.

'No. I'm not that low. I'm just telling the truth.'

At that very minute, a man with a massive beard and beads in his hands crept near them, then stood in front of them.

'What are you two doing?' he hissed. Sara knew he was a Dog, responsible for the chastity of the students.

'Nothing.' Sara murmured, not daring to look at the man.

'I have something to report,' Farzad declared. 'I've seen this student in a very inappropriate situation with one of our lecturers. And as a true Muslim and a decent student, I feel obliged to tell you, so you can end this disgrace. She's been insisting that I should not tell you.'

It seemed obvious to Sara that Farzad sounded spiteful and stupid, even to a chastity Dog. Besides, Farzad had no evidence. He was only putting himself in trouble.

'Tell me more.' The bearded man addressed Farzad while throwing a brief side-glance at Sara. Sara realised her scarf was in the middle of her head, exposing all her purple-dyed hair. And she knew her purple lip gloss was shining like a burning star: she'd spent so much time and thought, specifically picking it for her meeting with Dr Ahmadi.

'Who is he? Tell me the name of the lecturer.'

'But of course he's lying!' Sara was sure this was all a nightmare.

'The most disgraceful part is that ... I'm afraid, that lecturer is a lady.'

Sara saw something exploding in the eyes of the bearded man like thunderclouds, from under his bushy eyebrows. She felt sick with fear.

'Follow me,' he commanded. 'Both of you.'

Sara looked at Farzad desperately, but he avoided her eyes. Sara could feel now that he was determined to ruin her, and not just her. And she wanted to stop it, but did not know how.

At home she tried her best not to tell her mother that she'd missed her second class, due to being interrogated by The Dogs in a stall in the depths of the university. She did not want to tell her mother that she was on the verge of expulsion, that she'd lost to a loser like Farzad. That she was going to lose everything she'd worked so hard for. Everything her mother was proud of.

'Are you all right, darling?' Her mother asked her. 'Your face looks pale.'

'My face is always pale!' Sara tried to chuckle. But the

lump in her throat didn't allow it. The stench of the stall was still in her nostrils.

'You know you can tell me anything,' her mother reassured her. Sara knew this, but did not want to drag her down to her vulgar misery.

'I'm in trouble at uni,' she wept uncontrollably.

Her brother stepped in the living room from outside. 'What the hell has she done now?' he was sixteen, with a history of antagonising Sara since childhood.

'Go to your room,' her mother ordered him quietly.

'He's right. I'm a loser.'

'It's okay, darling. Whatever it is, we'll find a way to sort it out. Just tell me what it is.' Her mother embraced her.

Sara told her everything she could tell her. She told her nothing about her feelings for Dr Ahmadi. Only that she understood her art and regularly saw her outside of the classroom to give her more feedback, because she was a responsible tutor, who believed in her. She recounted Farzad's harsh romantic confession and his lies to The Dog. She told her mother about missing her second class – Human Figure 1 – due to being interrogated in a stall by a bearded Dog and a Dog in a chador. She said she was not upset, only furious. And she wept until she could not weep. She also confided she was worried about 'the kindly lecturer'.

'We can't worry about her. We should focus on your situation,' her mother stated. 'I shall talk to Simin. Don't say anything to your dad yet.' Sara didn't say that she had forgotten about the existence of her taciturn workaholic father a long time ago.

Simin, her mother's ancient friend who was the head of another department at their university was Sara's only hope.

'I feel I'm in a nightmare. Why is this happening to me?' Sara asked her mother, expecting an answer.

'I'll call Simin right now. Just don't worry,' her mother brought her a glass of water and picked up the phone.

After a week of locking herself in her tiny room, splashing colours on her canvases, Sara was informed that she could return to the university as before. Simin pulled some strings so Sara wasn't expelled, but she made an oath to the chief of the Dogs and was asked to keep a low profile. She could not wait to graduate.

Dr Ahmadi wasn't seen at the university anymore. They replaced her with a bearded man whose major was Islamic architecture. Nobody heard her energetic laugh resonating in the corridors or felt her smiles brightening up the class. Or saw her red locks streaming down her pale face like blood. There was no trace of her passionate words on Rodin, or her annoying favouritism towards Sara. Without her favourite lecturer, university was absurd.

Yet Sara did not stop calling or texting her. Tara Ahmadi was the only person to whom Sara sent a Happy New Year message, as soon as it was announced. Sara went through all the new year rituals without actually seeing or feeling anything. She helped her parents make a beautiful *haft sin* by putting all the main ingredients in elegant handmade blue saucers on the table in their living room: sumac, vinegar, two polished red apples and even a gold fish, and a volume of Hafez. The guests admired their *haft sin*. Sara received money and presents from her aunts and uncles, smiled and kissed them, embraced their children and grandchildren, feigned joy in family photos, sucked on salty and sour pistachios, but could not feel anything but the burning absence of Tara Ahmadi. The gold fish died, and she did not cry – unlike the previous times. Sara turned twenty and did not stop texting Tara. *You have every right to be angry at me, but please just let me know if you're okay ...* She told her mother about her guilty conscience. But nothing about her thwarted feelings and missed calls. Her sweetest dreams began to revolve around the destruction of Farzad, rather than licking Tara's slender fingers. But then again, she realised retribution wasn't necessary, as Farzad was already destroying himself with pot.

Sara and Sahar were friends with Maral and Ali again. The only thing they had in common was their abject animosity towards Farzad. After his accusations against Sara, he'd called Maral a 'stinky whore' in another altercation. Now he was their favourite joke, and favourite object of hatred. And he was missing almost all the classes.

Sara's whole body shivered every time Farzad was nearby, even though he'd never look at her or approach her. Her body would shake so violently she needed to immediately sit on a bench and close her eyes and imagine stabbing an empty canvas to be able to cool down. Her mother warned her that hatred was more damaging to herself than to Farzad. But Sara couldn't help it.

One day, towards the end of spring, when the weather was becoming summery and sweltering, Dr Ahmadi finally replied to one of her numerous apologetic text messages, saying briefly she'd like to meet her in a café somewhere distant from the university. Sara was ecstatic. She wanted to finally confess her feelings. She wanted to tell her how she'd loved her – not just as a lecturer, but a lover. She knew they would finally get together. That was the only reality.

They were supposed to meet on a Monday at four in the afternoon.

The café was far from her house, deep inside a greasy shopping mall in East Tehran. Sara paid for a cab, as she did not want to smell like buses and shared taxis when seeing her love after causing her to lose her job three long months before. At first she wore the reddest scarf she had, then changed it for a black one. Her make-up was minimal and she showered herself with her mother's Versace perfume. She wore a tight *manteau* and tried to feel like a conqueror. A café was even better than her stifling office at their suffocating university. She took three of the best paintings she'd made during those lost months to show them to Dr Ahmadi and decided that, if she admired them, Sara would say that they were painted for her. That they were hers. Like herself.

The café was a cage reeking of cigarette smoke. Dr Ahmadi was wearing a loose yellow shawl around her head, her red locks looking exactly like blood in contrast with the yellow. She was wearing a loose black *manteau* hiding her breasts. The café was hot, and she looked cold.

'Thanks for agreeing to meet me. I understand your anger at me. But I'd do anything to make it up to you.' Sara was hoping her 'anything' desire would be something sexual.

'I'm not angry at you,' she said coldly, 'I'm angry at the system, and at myself.'

'Why at yourself?' Sara exclaimed.

'For taking a student so seriously,' Tara stared into Sara's eyes. Sara realised why her friends used to say her gaze was 'creepy'.

Sara clasped her paintings on her lap under the table, as she suddenly concluded this was the real nightmare. This was the real damage Farzad had done – this was far worse than being interrogated and insulted by the Dogs in the stall.

'You're still a child. You all are,' Tara was not going to stop, 'My mistake was that I thought you were any different from the rest of the students. Now I don't even remember why I thought that.' Sara noticed the myriad wrinkles around her eyes for the first time, and was ready to be shot down by her. Dr Ahmadi's bullets were relentless now. 'Was it your looks? Your all-consuming paintings? Or the fact that you actually expressed interest in your major – unlike most of your peers.' Dr Ahmadi paused and Sara thought she'd finally shot her load, until she looked directly at Sara for the first time that evening and fired point blank, 'or the fact that you started manipulating me since the moment you saw me?' Tara raised her trembling voice. 'What did you want from me?' she paused to angrily unzip her black bag. Sara expected her to take out a gun, but instead she grabbed a Winston cigarette. Upon inhaling the smoke deeply, she lowered her voice, 'You were going to get the best grade anyway, you were already the top student, weren't you?' Sara was amazed at the fact that it never occurred to her that her miniature love was a smoker. And her smoking figure was the most torturously beautiful thing Sara had ever seen.

Sara knew Tara knew what she wanted and it wasn't a fucking grade. Dr Ahmadi had played along, too. Dr Ahmadi had approached her, too and had encouraged being approached by Sara. Dr Ahmadi had flirted back, had even initiated flirting herself. Just because she had paid a higher price, didn't mean she could blame Sara for everything. And Sara found this new game pretty violent. It seemed to Sara that Tara was just thirsty for a forbidden confession so she could weaponise that too. Sara suddenly realised that Tara even considered art a powerful weapon and nothing else. She rarely praised originality and technique as much as the power of a piece. She was always looking for the 'power' of a movement. 'Wherein lies the power of Dadaism?' Sara could now hear her again and see her clearly for the first time, writhing in sharp artworks, horny for power. *She should've studied politics or international relations, or anything else but art*, Sara thought, *art is as much about vulnerability as it is about power. And the distinction isn't even clear.* Instead of saying all this to her, Sara managed only to mumble, 'I'm sorry,' while staring down at the crooked metal ashtray on their tiny table.

Two other women were sitting at the nearest table to them, gossiping loudly about their mothers in law. Sara overheard one saying she had given up and was only praying to God for the removal of her mother-in-law from the face of the earth. At that moment, Sara would be happy to swap her place with any of them, even with their cursed mothers in law, even with the non-existent god.

'You have no idea how sorry I am,' she repeated herself.

'Don't be.' Tara said, smashing her third cigarette in the nasty ashtray, 'It wasn't really your fault.'

'It wasn't yours, either.' Sara managed to say, inhaling the remains of Tara's strong smoke.

'It doesn't matter anyway. I'm pleased you weren't

expelled. I mean if you look at it closely, we were lucky we weren't flogged. You know, your connection was a powerful one.'

'Yes, of course.' Sara let tears fill her eyes. She was tired of fighting them.

'Actually, I'm very happy these days,' Dr Ahmadi was staring at the space behind Sara.

'Oh, why is that?'

'Our application finally got accepted after almost five years. We're moving to Canada in a month.'

'We?'

'Me and my husband. I mean, I'm not even sorry I lost that exhausting job.'

Sara dried her tears. She could not wait to end this torment. She stood up. 'Can I leave now?'

'Of course. Can I just ask you to do me a favour?'

'Anything.' Suddenly Sara was willing to do 'anything' for Tara again.

'Can you stop bothering me, please? I have no interest in seeing you or hearing from you ever again. Good luck with painting, though. I still believe you're a real artist!'

Sara turned her back and left the café, grasping her paintings so hard they hurt her hands.

Shiraz Rains

L iving in Shiraz altered my life for good, despite the fact that I was homesick for my hometown, the Caspian Sea, and the rain.

To my family's pleasure, I had been accepted to study software engineering in the high-ranking University of Shiraz. At that time, I also wanted to get married, like my cousins. Everyone was trying to set me up with girls so that even I thought I wanted a girlfriend.

The first semester, every time I saw any slightly hand-some and friendly boy, I felt close to him. Since my puberty, I'd always been horny, praying to God to grant me a good wife to appease my hormones.

One day, feeling lonelier than usual, I sat in the univer-sity's eatery; a gentleman came in, a black Samsonite case in his hands. He was tall and had longish hair, like me. At that time this was a trend set by The Backstreet Boys. But he was not like any other man I had ever seen before. I couldn't stop staring at him, thinking, *this is how an engineer must look: handsome.*

On this winter day, as soon as I left the university, it

rained. And I felt so in love with the rain that I took off my coat to completely absorb each drop.

I was on my way to my dormitory, which was on a hill. The dorm was from the Pahlavi era, and was supposed to resemble the Shah's crown. I needed to get the bus in order to get there. I was standing there, drenched, ecstatic, waiting for the bus, when I realised someone was approaching me. It was the handsome guy I had seen in the canteen only a few minutes ago. He said, 'why are you standing in the rain like this? You'll catch a cold.'

'I'm from the north, and I miss home.' I said.

On the bus, we sat next to each other and I was trembling. I felt warm when he told me his name, Hasan.

'The name of our second Imam!' I said, giggling, heat coursing through my shivering body for inexplicable reasons.

He shrugged, 'yes,' his playful facial expression became suddenly solemn, 'maybe that is why he is my favourite Imam of all the twelve.'

My smile stopped too. It had never occurred to me to actually have, or pick, a 'favourite Imam'. It sounded like something my granny would say.

Interesting, I thought, and said, 'Where are you from?', which changed our conversation into something light and casual. Upon finding out that we were in the same building, he said, 'now that we live in the same place, you'll have to come over for tea!' I felt so excited I couldn't reply properly, just laughed and blushed.

He seemed like a traditional and religious man, very straight, and I was still hoping to fall for a girl. That night, still trembling on my duvet, I convinced myself that our encounter wasn't anything serious, just a chit-chat about our favourite Imams, we were just being friendly. It didn't mean anything at all.

The next day, after attending the university, I went out for a burger with my classmates, so I arrived in my room later in the evening. My flatmate informed me someone had been phoning our flat, looking for me every half an hour since morning. While I was changing into my pyjamas, Hasan called again. This time, I answered, my heart thumping. Hasan was asking me to go over to his. I found my cleanest shirt, slicked my hair back, showered myself with my flatmate's cologne, and sauntered out of our room.

His room was at the end of our building, and he had the whole space to himself. The room was rather spacious, with a small desk placed under one of the windows. The windows opened to the magnificent lights of Shiraz in the evening, twinkling, full of promise. I could not help but notice that there was only a slight distance between the two single beds.

To my disappointment, there were other people in his room, sitting on the floor. I sat beside them, leaning on the metal frame of one of the beds, facing Hasan's beauty. We had tea and talked. One of his guests was a poet. They were all Lor ethnicity and we talked only about poetry, *she'er*. Hasan had interesting opinions. Like our styles, our tastes in literature were opposite; he was into classical literature, Hafez and Saadi, but I was into Forough and Sohrab. I never thought I could even enjoy the company of someone who disregarded modern poetry, yet I found myself strangely aroused when Hasan opposed contemporary literature, and viewed only classical works as true literature. This was only a glimmer of his personality. Later on, I realised that we were like fire and ice in every aspect of life, from food, to dressing, to dealing with family and friends.

Unlike me, he seemed like a traditional man, from a very traditional family. Even though I also used to pray and *namaz*, I looked like a total *soosool*, with my blue jeans and polished silver Nike trainers. Hasan always wore formal suits.

Despite these fundamental differences, we were with each other night and day. In classes, in the canteen, at the university, in the dormitory. We meticulously arranged to do everything with each other. Our tastes in music were also the opposite. I liked Western pop music, and he traditional Iranian music. We tried to merge our tastes. He became a bit modern, and I a bit traditional. The first time I arrived home since befriending Hasan, my sister remarked the change, laughing 'why have you become so *ommol*?!'

When we were at the dormitory, I was mostly in Hasan's room. Every night we lay on the two beds, talking. On one of these nights, listening to pop music on Radio Farda, I told Hasan I liked a girl in our university; upon uttering these words, the electricity in the building was suddenly cut off, and we lay in the dark, listening to each other breathing, the flow of our conversation interrupted. Hasan coughed, and I heard the fabric of his clothes brush against the sheet. The next thing I knew, he was lying next to me, our bodies touching each other. The racing of my heart was uncontrollable. He told me I was too young to have a girlfriend, he reasoned that it was even early for him, who was two years my senior. We talked about love in the dark until my mouth went dry. I was shamefully aroused. I realised I didn't have any feelings for that girl at all and all I ever wanted was Hasan. I lay there, anxious that someone might walk in and discover us, and I was worried and aroused until the lights came back on.

When they did, the radio filled the room with intolerably loud music. I felt blinded by the lights. I jumped, so he wouldn't see my arousal. I glanced at his crotch and realised he was even more aroused than I. We both sat on the edge of the bed, and I swiftly kissed his cheekbones, saying, 'thanks for listening to me.'

This was the starting point of many nights of us sleeping in the same bed. Yet we still did not touch each other sexually. We'd just embrace, fully clothed. Sometimes he dropped his head on my shoulders. We didn't care about people seeing us in the same bed. Sometimes, when we were in my room, my flatmate would barge in, pretending he hadn't seen us, immediately leaving upon finding me and Hasan on my bed.

One day, Hasan told me he needed to travel to the Holy Mashhad as he had a *nazr* of visiting the holy shrine of Imam Reza for being accepted in a *sarasari* university. So, we travelled to Mashhad together. We travelled by train, changing at Tehran, sitting opposite each other with three other people in our carriage. We both pretended to look at the view through the windows, but all I could see and feel was Hasan's dark glances on my face. Sometimes I returned them, other times I was too afraid and flustered to do anything.

After checking into our three-star hotel, we went straight to our room to get rid of our rucksacks. I still remember our room number, thirty-six. When I was changing out of the T-shirt I had worn on the train, and Hasan was on his way to take a shower, a white towel wrapped around his thin waist, our bare shoulders briefly touched, the spot crackling with strange electricity.

A few minutes later, when we were in the gilded holy shrine, engulfed by its enormity, I felt terribly guilty and I could tell Hasan was feeling the same. By this time, I was certain that he desired what I desired, but we just could not act upon our desires.

Strolling in an empty alleyway on our way back to the hotel, my hand knocked against his and his fingers curled around mine: he squeezed and I squeezed back. My whole body warmed up, as if I had been touching a heater in winter. All I could think about was room thirty-six and the terrifying and yet thrilling inevitability of what was about to happen between us.

In our cheap hotel, we tore off each other's clothes, letting our underpants stay on, we madly kissed each other's bodies until I finally dared to take his underpants off, and he mine, and we burst in each other's burning mouths.

The first words he said after he came were, 'I hope God forgives us, there isn't any sin left for us to do!'. But there was.

After that night we slept beside each other naked, every night. Yet we wouldn't penetrate each other, as it was the ultimate sin.

After returning to Shiraz, we requested to be in the same flat, and they accepted.

*

The moment we moved in together, we had penetrative as well as oral sex every night and day. My whole existence was nothing but love for him. I didn't think about anyone else. I had a feeling that we would stay with each other for ever. I worried when he returned home late. I was jealous of all the other men who existed in the world, even our mutual friends. We fought. After our classes, I was just waiting for him to come home. He came home at night. My favourite thing to do was to pretend that I was asleep, so he'd touch me more. The first six months we fought over the smallest matters. After six months, we suddenly stopped fighting, and I let myself drown in our beautiful calm sea.

But after two years, our sex dramatically decreased and I couldn't feel his warmth anymore; I feared he was becoming cold.

One night, we fought and I accused him of seeing someone else. We broke every plate and lamp in sight, yet we were careful not to hit each other. Hasan pulled a piece of paper from his drawer and disappeared. I had no news from him until the day after. The next night, when he arrived back at our flat, he didn't tell me where he had been. I was dying to know. I fumbled in his pockets and found the piece of paper. A love letter from a girl, called Zeinab. Our majestic castle shattered. When I asked him whether or not he was exchanging love letters with his cousin, Zeinab, he denied it, but after I waved the letter in his furious face, he confessed, saying he needed to get married to a woman eventually, because of his mother.

'I'll be with you until I get married,' he added, 'but afterwards we shall separate.' It was at that moment that I decided to break up with him. And I did. Except that he prevented me from going through with it by crying and kissing me.

I stayed, but my love turned into hate. I was just waiting to graduate in a few months and to leave Shiraz for good. I didn't have sex with him anymore, despite his insistence.

During my last week in Shiraz, not having sex with me was killing him. He was unstoppable; he even tried to seduce me in a friend's place, but I wouldn't accept it. On the day of my departure, he was constantly tearful, and when we reached the bus stop, he burst into hysterical sobs. It was at that moment that I experienced emotional paralysis for the first time in my life. I felt nothing and said nothing and, at the same time, I was worried that if I opened my mouth even slightly, the universe would explode.

Back in my parents' house in Saari, I was anything but happy. In fact, I was aware that I was massively depressed. I took long walks on the beach every night, awaiting my ferociously gorgeous Caspian to evoke some life-giving feelings inside me. But the sea had never seemed so ruthless and hollow.

Using the dial-up internet, I searched, and realised there were many people like me. I stumbled upon a few blogs written by these people; they wrote about their emotions. These blogs became my therapy. I chatted with those familiar strangers. I realised what it meant to be gay, I found a definition. This new definition revived me to the point where I ended up attending the entrance exam to continue my studies and I got accepted to do my Master's at the University of Tehran.

*

In Tehran, I lived alone, I was depressed, and became bald. Day and night, I distracted myself with my studies and my blog, called Utopia, in which I posted my immature poems and wrote about my emotions and adventures with Hasan. In a strange way, I released the fervour of my feelings into both engineering and blogging. Until one day, I received an invitation to his wedding.

Upon receiving the ominous invitation, I sent him the link to my blog. He called me afterwards, telling me that he still loved me, that he'd told his wife I was just a close friend and he kept my pictures. He proposed that I settle in Isfahan, and become his neighbour so he could be both married and in a relationship with me. His tears echoed through the dark tunnel between us all the way to my Nokia handset. A ray of light. I booked a ticket to fly to Isfahan in order to attend his wedding.

When I arrived in Isfahan, instead of visiting its famous monuments like a normal tourist, I spent my free hour before the wedding masturbating madly to gay porn, in the hope of not desiring him upon seeing him in his black groom attire. However, when I got to the wedding salon, the men's section, one mutual glance from afar was enough to dump me back in those love-painted days in Shiraz. After that one painfully powerful glance, we both looked away. He shook hands with an older man, possibly his future wife's father − not that it mattered − and I looked around, attempting to appreciate the beauty I was surrounded by: handsome men, all in dark suits, smiling, all looking alike, all looking like Hasan, yet very different from him. He stood out, not as the handsome groom, but as the love of my life, the only man I had ever wanted.

I was contemplating the easiest way to escape while eating silent tears, which were making my eyes hot and itchy, when one of the handsome men approached me. He looked younger than me and Hasan, early twenties, with big beautiful teeth that made his smile even more stunning, he looked like Hasan when we were young in Shiraz and not yet wrinkled by life. He softly shook my hand, saying his name, which immediately escaped my mind, but it wasn't Hasan, and offered me alcohol under his breath, bringing his mouth closer to mine. I could smell the alcohol on his youthful breath. I ended up drinking so much Aragh that I don't remember anything else. By the end of the night, I found myself in a car, with a few people attempting to sober me up. To my relief, the alcohol angel was gone.

The next day, in my painful hangover on the stuffy plane back to the greyness of Tehran, I decided to cut Hasan out of my life. For good.

Two years later, when I finished my Master's and was working as a well-paid engineer, Hasan came to Tehran for the book fair, and of course, he stayed with me. I was a serial dater.

We went to the book fair, and purchased Proust's *In Search of Lost Time*, following the recommendation of some of my blog commentators.

When we returned to my flat, we threw the plastic bags of books to the floor, and Hasan threw himself on my double bed, moaning about the traffic. I sat on the edge of the bed, looking into his eyes, seeing his willingness and I was thrown back to six years ago. I found it unsettling that my feelings towards him had barely altered. He closed his eyes, his lips ready to be kissed. I could not resist and before we knew it, we were entangled. However, even though I was full of pleasure, I couldn't block the mental image of his wife. I also felt he was feeling guilty, I tried to take it slow, but he wanted to end it faster. I was trying to prolong the fellatio as much as possible. When it came to the intercourse, I wanted it to last forever, taking it slow and steady, but he forced us to end it quicker by saying, 'That's enough, let's finish!' and we fucked till we both came. In an instant, he banged the door shut, and I felt as alone as ever, as if he had never been there.

Acid

A man is running after me through the tree-lined streets, near my parents' house in Shiraz. There is a bottle of acid in his hands. I am running so swiftly I am almost flying. I had no idea I could run so fast. But the man is even faster, and he is closer to me now. Then, an explosion inside my body, and I wake up. My torso twitches, and I realise that I am in my dark room in London. I turn on the lights, blinding myself for a moment. Still, it's better than being attacked by that man. It's five in the morning. I know it must be around nine o'clock in Iran, therefore my mother must be awake. I call her.

'I read about the acid attacks on women with *bad hejab*,' I tell her, trying to sound cool, like a reporter. But I am a terrible actor; my voice shivers.

'Honey, I know you're worried now. They're probably just rumours . . . and in Isfahan, not Shiraz.'

'They're not rumours. The police have confirmed four of the cases,' I say. 'Mum, could you please wear a chador when you go out?'

My mother laughs. 'I was actually grateful for the first

time that you're not here ... their main focus is on the youth. They wouldn't bother with an oldie like me.'

'But you're still stunning, and your *hejab* is awful.'

'What's the point of you living abroad when all you do is read the Iranian news and obsess about it? How are your studies going? How's your beautiful boyfriend?'

When I fall asleep again, I dream of our house in Shiraz, with my father's antiques adorning the living room, and my mother's elegant bookshelves. There are numerous photographs of my sister and me in burnished wooden frames all over the walls, as though we were dead. Perhaps we are dead to them, since we only get to meet them three weeks a year, when we go back to Shiraz for our holidays. My sister flies all the way from Lyon, and I from London. Every time we gather, each of us has grown a year older. Last time I was there, I realised my father couldn't go mountain climbing anymore. And my mother can only read with glasses now.

Last week, my father turned sixty-nine. As soon as I saw his old face, all blurry on Skype, I decided not to say *'Tavalodet Mobarak'*, because I didn't want to burst into tears in front of him. He was looking pleased. My mother had bought him a fancy watch, and he showed it to me, happy as a child with a new doll. I wanted to hold him. I wanted to hold him for good. Thank goodness, Skype cut off due to their slow internet. And now Skype has completely vetoed Iran. We will have to find a new way to see them.

My sister and I usually discuss what we will do when our parents are really old and in need of assistance. The thought of my parents, still so full of life, being old and frail one day pains me. Parents should never get old.

As I brush my teeth, I try my best to think of beautiful things in my life – like James.

It is ten in the morning. I have decided to avoid the internet for a day in order to study and do a news–detox. I realise with pleasure I have to read 'The Love Song of J. Alfred Prufrock' in preparation for our class.

I take a shower, and then boil some milk to drink with honey. James calls me to confirm that we are meeting his friends tonight at a pub in Angel.

I am quite anxious. Till now, I haven't been capable of dating anyone long enough to meet their friends. But I've been going out with James for four months now. I have decided to go out with him and only him for 'the rest of my life'.

'What if your friends don't approve of me?' I ask him, trying to put on my cool reporter's voice. It seldom works, but I've decided not to give up hope and practice. I know one day I will succeed. One victorious day, my voice will be cold and steady, dripping with nonchalance, enabling me to wish my father a happy birthday on Skype or on another app that has not proscribed Iran.

'They will. They're awesome, and you're adorable,' he informs me in his BBC accent. His voice has a certain kind of coldness that burns me.

He has told me before that his friends are like his family – he doesn't have much of a family. His father was a priest who seduced a nun, abandoning her when she fell pregnant with James in order not to lose his priesthood. James believes his father is a 'bastard', pronouncing the word so violently it almost sounds German. His intonation then is gloriously ruthless, almost lascivious.

It is three in the afternoon and I'm lethargic, having done some translation and transcribing work in exchange for some meagre pennies, so I decide to make tea. I put two spoons of loose black tea in the fiery red teapot, and break three sticks of cinnamon and a pod of cardamom. This is the way my father makes tea. My father despises teabags, considers them a 'cancerous conspiracy' by tasteless teabag corporations that have no humanity. My sister and I used to mock him for this when we still lived in Shiraz, but after years of being apart, we have grown to feel as offended as he does by teabags.

James is half an hour late, as usual. I don't want to drink my tea without him, so I wolf down a blueberry muffin. Then I put on some mascara and sweet-tasting lip gloss. I don't bother wearing clothes, as I know they'll be taken off as soon as he arrives.

He knocks on the door, and I feel my heart jump about in my chest like a demented bird. I am already wet.

When I open the door, he barges in, drenched by the London weather, his golden locks plastered darkly to his scalp. We don't talk, only kiss for I don't know how long. Then I grab his hands and lead him to my bedroom, pushing him on my waiting bed.

We stare into each other's eyes and I bite his hard nipples. James moans and when I thrust his hard penis into my wet vagina, I forget about everything.

It is this state of amnesia that I like most about sex – second to the orgasm of course. I forget about Isfahan, acid attacks, my parents' age, the US-imposed sanction paralysing Iran, exploitative translation work, how much I've missed my sister since the last time she came to London a few months ago. I even forget about the right way to make tea. I also forget about the Islamic State, and the fact that they are nearing Iran's borders, sworn to Allah to behead each and every Shia on their way. I wonder if they'd feel calmer if we told them that many of us are avid atheists, not exactly Shias. Having sex also helps me forget that one of my Syrian friends told me she hoped the Sunni extremists or the American army would 'save' Syria by dethroning Asad. I was shocked at these horrifying ways of being rescued, but I didn't feel I had the right to say anything. I just looked into her dark eyes, and told her how sorry I was that our government was supporting Assad. She'd told me before that Syrians hated Iranians because of that.

Amidst our moans and groans, I hear the sound of ceramic shattering. I remember I left the teapot on the stove. My poor teapot!

James is staring into my eyes with his slanted blue ones. 'What is it?'

'It doesn't matter,' I keep riding him.

After writhing on my black sheets, we lie immobile, both breathless. James checks his phone. 'It's half past five,' he announces, as though I'd asked the time.

'What time are we meeting your friends?'

'Sixish.'

I reluctantly leave his body, and the bed. I know my hair and make-up are a mess and need fixing. James looks perfect and I feel a kind of sorrow that his beauty is untouched and untouchable.

'By the way, what happened to that Syrian friend of yours? When is she coming to London?' James asks, while

I'm looking at my funny hair in the mirror. 'What was her name again?'

'Lubna,' I say, and the ecstasy of our sex escapes me. 'She's not coming.'

'Oh, why?' James asks. I get the impression he's feeling rather pleased about this. One time, he confessed he was jealous of Lubna, when I made the mistake of telling him that Lubna and I had sex a few times. And it was 'divine'.

'Her visa got rejected again.' I try to console myself by adding, 'but she's safe. She's settled down in Istanbul now.'

I put on my black bra and knickers and have no idea what else to wear for this important occasion. 'What should I wear?'

'You'd look good in anything,' James tells me as he joins me in front of the mirror. We look at our reflection and smile. 'Alex is going to be so jealous! He competes with me on the sly, and he's single at the moment.' James's voice is excited – especially compared to his usual, composed tone.

'Perhaps he's chosen to be single. What's wrong with that?' I blurt out, regretting it the moment the words leave my big mouth. And yet I cannot stop, 'I used to enjoy being single ... from time to time. Relationships can feel suffocating at times.'

James does not say anything. I sort of pity him. He is like a tender rose. I embrace him, aching to tell him I am miserably in love with him, but, like Prufrock, I am unable to confess my love.

'What I'm trying to say is I might not be Alex's type ... he might not find me attractive.' I am struggling to find the right English words.

'You're unambiguously beautiful. And exotic! He'll be

very jealous!' James smiles. I am happy about his happiness; I just hate it when people exoticise me as if I were a rare plant, not just another dysfunctional human.

I put on a purple tank top with a black mini skirt. 'What do you think?'

'Stunning,' James puts his delicate hands around my shoulders. 'Shall we go now?'

'One moment . . . just let me emphasise my orgasm . . .' Saying this, I add some blush on my cheeks.

James smirks, but looks at his mobile.

'You look ready now . . .' he almost begs.

'One moment, honey,' I carefully put on a violet lip gloss. I decide not to wear any perfume; I want to preserve his scent on my skin.

'Do you always take so long to get ready?' he asks.

'Oh my god, you're killing me! Let's go!'

I look at him, expecting him still to be naked. Apparently, he put on his clothes while I was putting on make-up. I kill my desire for dramatising his beauty with make-up. Our last argument is still ringing in my ears, 'Please don't forget I'm a man!' he'd defeated me with his insurmountable logic.

He is wearing a white and yellow striped shirt with black skinny jeans. I'm allergic to the colour, but in yellow James looks like the sun. I look at his long, slim legs and I am ready to fuck him again and again, never leaving the bed.

'Ah, don't give me that look! They're waiting for us!'

'What look?' I take my purse.

We take the Northern line and get off at Angel. 'Is there anything you need to tell me?'

'Well,' James declares. 'You know I *love* how opinionated you are, and I do like your political arguments, but . . .'

I cannot imagine what he is about to tell me, and I'm used to being called 'opinionated' by my English acquaintances. I try to think of a Farsi equivalent for this strange word, but I cannot come up with anything. ' . . . As you know, Sarah is a devout Muslim and Alex is a Christian white man – like me; could you please not discuss the oppressiveness of religion, racism, and sensitive subjects like that?'

I wonder if that's how I appear to him: jumping desperately onto every opportunity to 'discuss sensitive subjects'.

'Well, I won't,' I say. 'Unless they ask my opinion on something.' I keep reminding myself that I have to be careful not to hurt James, that he is a tender flower I love too much to harm, that he is more important to me than any political stance I might hold.

'Well, even if they pressed you – Alex might do that, actually – perhaps don't even say outright that you're an atheist.'

'What's wrong with being an atheist?' I exclaim.

'There's nothing wrong with it. But, you do know I'm from a Catholic background? My friends are believers, especially Sarah who just converted to Islam. She's fun though. You'll love her.'

The pub looks like any other British pub: mahogany, sweltering, and noisy. I suppose I should be grateful that there's no giant TV exploding with football and red-faced hooligans, and that it's not a quiz night.

I look around to spot his friends. He has so many friends,

but tonight 'only six' of them are coming; his besties being Sarah and Alex.

It is not difficult to recognise them, even though I have never met them before. The only white woman in a complete *hejab* is obviously Sarah, sitting beside a stylish black woman. From James, I know that this woman 'used to be a handsome man, called Paul'. Now she is Yasmine.

Yasmine greets us warmly. Alex pretends he hasn't seen us, even though he is sitting right in front of us. Sarah is staring at her iPhone as if it were a rare species, and she a scientist.

I sip my beer slowly, careful not to get drunk and say something feminist, political, postcolonial, anti-religious, lustful, atheistic, or generally destructive to my lover's friends. I try to be as well-behaved as possible, so I paste a smile onto my face.

Yasmine is the only one who speaks to me. She asks what I'm doing in London. She says she's also studied English literature, and compliments my English. She is my favourite. We bond over Prufrock. And she shows me a poem on her phone by her favourite poet that I haven't heard of before: Danez Smith. I keep reading Yasmine's favourite poem. It makes me tremble; I have never read a poem like that before. I was never taught this poem. Perhaps, I can muster the courage to ask our tutors to teach us this instead of William Carlos Williams' plums and wheels for the thirtieth time.

I sip my beer, and stare at Yasmine. I confess to myself that she is the most beautiful woman I have ever seen in my life. She has the large, piercing, dark-brown eyes of Lubna. Like her, Yasmine's also painted her lips neon red. I drink my beer and feel like I need something stronger. I wish I could stop staring at Yasmine.

I know Lubna hates my guts, because I left something special in search of something much less special. Yasmine catches my eyes, I look down and I am sure I am blushing. She politely smiles, then looks away.

Then, I feel the glancing blow of eyes on me – Sarah's heavy gaze. She is scrutinising my cleavage, then the length of my mini skirt. I know my style isn't justified for her, as a white woman's would be. James has told her about my background and nationality. I know she knows that when a Muslim drinks alcohol, it's not the same as a white person drinking alcohol. That when a Muslim is wearing revealing clothes, it's much worse than a white woman in such garments. It has a meaning. It is an obnoxious statement.

Her *hejab* resembles that of the so-called 'sisters' of the morality police in Iran. If she were living in Iran, she probably wouldn't have to worry about being attacked by acid. The combination of her whiteness and having chosen Islam would make her a national hero. I can imagine our authorities ejaculating on our national TV channels for this chaste woman who chose the right path herself – without coercion. In fact, she could get a well-paid government job, and freely reprimand women who dress even one tenth as outrageously as I am dressed now. She would marry a bearded hezbollah with plastic rosary beads in his large, hairy hands. They would produce six children, who would behave exactly like them, only one of them would be a closeted homosexual, who would end up hanging themselves in the bathroom when the rest of their family were praying at the mosque.

I smile at Sarah and curse myself for being so paranoid and judgmental. I tell myself that Sarah would probably face issues in Iran, as she is Sunni. That Sarah has nothing to do with the morality police. She is a lovely friend of my love, and she likes me. James told me before that he'd shown my picture to Sarah and she said I was 'super pretty'. Oh, thank god almighty.

I start to feel rather silly for carrying on smiling at Sarah, when she obviously has no desire to speak to me. So I try my luck with Alex, but receive the same reaction from him. I ask Yasmine the name of her dog. I say it's a charming name, even though I'm not sure if I heard it correctly. James touches my right thigh surreptitiously under the table and I feel alive. That is the whole point.

Three of the friends who were mostly talking to James leave. It is now only me, James, Yasmine, Sarah, and Alex.

James addresses Sarah, 'You've been staring at your phone the whole time!'

Sarah finally looks up and stares hard at him. 'I'm mad at you.' She slurps her orange juice and looks at me. I have accepted the pathetic fact that I am frightened of her.

She is giving James a complicated reason as to why she is angry with him. I've had too much beer to be able to concentrate – or care, or understand my second language. I catch Alex staring at me and give him my useless smile that I'm getting sick of. I want to go home with James, just the two of us. I want to embrace him and confess my love. I don't want to be Prufrock, I want to be Oscar Wilde; but not in front of Sarah and Alex.

Yasmine is saying goodbye. I want to beg her not to leave. I won't. She leaves. Part of me is praying that I will see her again. I catch Alex gazing at me. Sarah is laughing hysterically at something James is telling her. Apparently, her problem with him has been sorted out. I try to make small talk with Alex, which turns into a long chat about music. But the moment I mention Oasis' 'Slide Away', the acoustic version, as one of my all-time favourite songs, Alex informs me that my knowledge of 'British bands' is making him feel 'strange' and he nervously laughs. I shut up, as I don't know what to say, and don't know why I feel insulted, and don't know why I want to go home on my own. He kills the awkward silence by asking me about my favourite Persian food. I reply 'aubergine stew', in order not to be a bitch. He says I have to cook for him sometime. I inform him that I am a terrible chef. James narrows his beautiful eyes at Alex, as though in comic rage towards him. I almost chuckle. Sarah laughs too. She is suddenly giving me a sweet smile. I smile back, pathetically relieved.

'I've heard so many nice things about you,' I tell her, my voice so shrill and sycophantic it hurts. And for a second I forget where I am physically. I am thrown back into one of those dark, cosy, smoked-up, cinnamon-scented cafés in the middle of Shiraz with my own friends and we are laughing at nothing. And then Lubna enters the hostel in Istanbul. For the first two hours, we talk nonstop about Iran and Syria, and Lubna says she can imagine why many Iranians hate Islam. I stare into her eyes, saying, I do not hate Islam; I dislike all religions, and all authorities. She takes my hand and the next thing I know we are walking in Taksim square at seven in the evening, shopping, but not really. We are too broke and too horny. We go to an LC Waikiki and everything looks the same. Lubna tries on a cheap, orange top and asks my opinion. We stare at each other for what feels like a century. Under Galata tower at midnight, she kisses me and I lick off all her red lipstick. I still recall its bittersweet taste, and Lubna's strong grip on my body. Whenever I think about this, my body still burns.

When I come back to my reality in London, I shiver with a strange sense of nostalgia that I hope I will get used to someday.

'Same, hon!' Sarah smiles again. I feel awful for having made assumptions about her. James was right. Sarah is a sweetheart, and like many young Iranians, I am suffering from what they call 'Islamophobia' in the West. It's not Sarah's fault that I am so fucked-up, caught between the lives I cannot even live, just to miss and to mourn.

'It's very interesting you're from Iran,' Sarah declares.

I keep smiling, but I don't know what to say. I can't see what's 'interesting' about that. But she is not awaiting a response. She exclaims, 'I bet you can't dress like this over there!' her smile still wide and bright. For a moment, I hope I've heard her wrong, lost in my tragic nostalgia. And yet I am aware I have not. She glances at my décolletage again, then stares into my eyes and smiles once more, her teeth sharp and large like a weapon. I feel tongue-tied. A second wave of shock captures me when I hear Alex and James laughing at her comment. And the third wave of shock sickens me as I hear myself snicker uncomfortably and say, 'No, I can't.' But after uttering 'can't', I forget how to speak English. My body saves me; I need to vomit, so I manage to mumble an apology and rush off to the bathroom.

While puking, I realise I am tipsy. I urinate forcefully, hoping the urine will scald my thighs.

Washing my mouth and hands, I look at my reflection in the mirror. I pull up my top to cover my cleavage. I look ill. I reapply my lip gloss, but its fruity taste makes me feel sicker. I leave my hands under the hot water for a few minutes. I'm hoping they have left. I want to go back to my place, with or without James. Now my only priority is escape – as it has always been. Also, I'm burning with a dangerous desire to get back at Sarah. 'Yes, you're right. Thanks to the religion of peace and your country's nonstop meddling, bullying, and manipulation, I can't dress the way I please in my country.' Now that I am recovering from my initial shock, I feel I am capable of fighting. I feel strong, like Lubna. However, I know if I succumb to that temptation, I will lose James.

They have not left. They're still there, but to my relief, Alex and Sarah are blanking me again. I sit beside James, and try to feel good despite everything. His youthful face is glowing in the pub light. He is terribly pretty. I want to kiss his little mouth vigorously, but I don't. I just put my hand on his thin thighs in his fine skinny jeans, like Lubna used to put hers on mine. Somebody leaves the door of the pub open and the London night air attacks us. I feel cold, so I put on my coat. James suddenly interrupts Sarah and asks me anxiously, 'Are you leaving?'

'Nope, just cold,' I reassure him, suddenly wondering if Lubna will accept me again if I move to Istanbul.

'Good, because I'd like to spend the night with you, if you're up for it.' He gives me one of his shining smiles while narrowing his eyes. I am pleased that I didn't play Sarah's vulgar game.

'I'd love that,' I admit, thinking that Lubna won't accept

me, because I, the fabulous idiot, have the habit of burning all my bridges.

Alex and Sarah leave at ten. I can't believe they're finally gone; this must be a dream.

As soon as they leave, James and I embrace each other and make out in the pub. He disrupts our kisses by asking me, 'Did you have fun?'

'Well . . .' I try to lie, but I can't. Instead I say, 'I would bear anything for you.'

He laughs and kisses me some more. 'You know what Sara told me when you went to the loo?'

I feel alarmed. 'What?' I am, after all, a godless slut. A heathen. A brown bitch with an alcoholic cleavage.

'She said you're as beautiful as your photo,' James snickers. 'She said she was pleased your picture wasn't photoshopped.'

'Oh, how sweet of her!' I suppose I should be laughing at her terribly witty comment too, but I can't. And I won't. In fact, I'm about to ask why it's any concern of hers how I 'really' look. After all, I'm not sleeping with her. With the help of my meagre self-control, I manage not to say this to James.

'I told you she's sweet!' James says. 'But you weren't really in the mood for socialising tonight, were you?'

'I wasn't?'

'You talked quite a bit with Yasmine, though.'

I don't know what to say. I'm sipping from my third pint of London Pride, thinking pride is something I haven't felt in ages, and London is something I constantly feel: it is cold. I am inebriated and do not feel like talking about trivial matters. And yet, how torturously and tragically I want James. Even though I have him, I feel it's inadequate and dissatisfying. Our love feels incomplete, fragile, and cold – even wrong, at times. It is good, but it is not what I could have had with Lubna. Even though James is prettier than Lubna, he doesn't have *that*. By *that*, I don't mean a vagina. However, I do not know what I mean. Or perhaps, it is just impossible to say what I mean.

We are walking to his flat in King's Cross. The air is crisp. We are both intoxicated. We hold on to each other so as not to fall down. We don't talk while walking.

So, I finally met his friends. But he will never see mine, even though I have informed them of James's significant existence. My mind flies to my friends in Shiraz. I think of our gatherings. I think of how we poured homemade wine on each other's chests and licked it under the pretext of playing 'Truth or Dare'. The truth is, there was no truth: it was only dare.

I am shuddering. I am in love with London, but I suddenly feel like leaving it. And yet, I dread the idea of living in Iran again, despite the fact that I know I will never find somewhere as beautiful as Shiraz in spring. My sister keeps telling me '*Faranseh* is so you' and calls England 'the arrogant colony of *Amrika*' in a haughty tone. I actually fancy going to France to live with my sister. Since she has finalised her divorce, she has become free again. We will listen to French music, watch French films, eat French cheese, drink French wine, and fuck French guys. And the tedious French classes my mother coerced me into taking will finally prove of use. I could continue my studies there. Perhaps, my sister can even find me an office job at the university where she teaches. I am certain it is easy to pretend to love Paris, to even die for it. That's what all the clichés say. The same clichés that say 'I Love London' with badly-painted hearts on cheap t-shirts bleeding all over Trafalgar Square. And the same clichés that say, 'Leave Iran and never look back!' but no matter how hard you try, once you have tasted Iran, you are addicted. You cannot not look back. And you will return every summer, and every Christmas, and every Persian New Year, and every bloody holiday. And your less wealthy and less successful friends who are still stuck in the process of escape will ask you, 'Why the hell do you keep coming back here? What is wrong with you? Why don't you go to Bali and Venice for holidays? To Paris and Berlin? There is nothing to see here.' And you don't even get their point anymore, despite the fact that you used to speak exactly like them, you can't even understand your mother tongue, because a traveller finally loses all her languages. And it dawns on me that I shall leave London like I left Shiraz. But what about James? The one and only James. My love, my rapture, my torment.

His bed is unmade, as always. We lie beside each other, not touching. I start biting his soft neck.

'Ouch!' he blurts out. I have no idea how to temper the pressure of my teeth on his skin, how to make it hurt less. Lubna and I bit each other, hard and a lot. It never hurt. I stop biting him. I still want to tell him how I feel about him. I want to tell him that my feelings towards him aren't a positive thing, because they're strangling me. I cannot breathe or focus whenever he is near me or whenever he is not with me; I am constantly restless and breathless and I no longer know how to contain myself. I want to tell him

I haven't felt this weak in ages and abhor this weakness, no matter how rapturous it is. His love makes me weak, while Lubna's made me strong. Why?

While I am licking his neck, like a desperately faithful dog, he sings these amorous words to me in his BBC accent: 'You should've talked more to Sarah. It was slightly awkward when you dashed off to the loo, just when she was warming up to you.'

I feel paralysed, physically and mentally. Part of me is hoping I am hallucinating. But as soon as James continues his sermon and analysis, I know I am not.

'Darling, I understand you. And I understand how you feel about religion, especially Islam. And it's completely understandable because you've been hurt. However, you do know that theocracy isn't necessarily representative of religion?'

I realise my cheeks are wet under my quiet tears. I am glad the room is dark so James cannot see my tears. He sounds too absorbed in his speech to notice anyway. 'You do realise how your government acts, or how ISIS does, has nothing to do with real Islam or creationism or whatever?'

I struggle to tell him he is right; that how his priest father acted had nothing to do with Christianity either. That he knows religion better than I do. That he knows what 'real' Islam is and I do not. I, who know the Quran by heart. I, born and raised in the Islamic Republic of Iran. I, who lost my country to Islam – and not just a country, but the whole of the Middle East. I, who have to celebrate my father's birthdays on Skype, and count the days, the months, the years just to drink tea with my mother and walk beside my sister. I, who left all my belongings and friends behind to survive – and yes, some of them drowned while I clung to a broken board and sadly survived. I, who can see the women of my country disfigured, mutilated and destroyed by acid and yet nobody is allowed to object, or even 'question' and everybody has to be horribly cautious not to 'disrespect' anyone's religious beliefs. I who can neither forgive nor forget, and yet I am too exhausted to fight or even hope. I know I have lost Lubna to religion, too. We were both laughing when we promised not to fall in love, despite *that*. Whatever that was.

'My religious mother would execute me if she finds out what we do!' Lubna sometimes said, laughing. I have not seen her in two years now. But her laughter still rings in my ears. And I hope her mother survived America's bombs, because Lubna was worried about her not ever being able to leave Syria. Where was James then to teach us a lesson or two?

When I was at school, choked by my tight *hejab*, chanting *Ayatolkorsi* every day at seven in the morning under the scorching sun, James was drugged and drunk, shaking his perfect little arse in some rainy rock 'n' roll festival. And don't even get me started on Ramadan. Yes, of course he should teach me a thing or two about Islam. After all, he has a 'sweet' Muslim friend and a degree from SOAS.

'I care about you ... a lot. So we should do something about your phobias.' James holds me. I stay motionless like a log.

I feel I am nothing. He is absolutely right. It is not just Islam. It is also America and its aggressive obsession with Iran, its deathly sanctions. It is Christianity and its homophobic soldiers. It is Netanyahu exploiting our every mishap to push a point. It is misogyny. It is patriarchy. It is heterosexual rules. It is his white saviour complex. It is him controlling my social behaviour. His missionary attitude. It is everything that stinks and I cannot do anything about it apart from mourning and getting more bitter and nostalgic as I age. I feel poisoned.

He holds me tighter in the dark. 'I like how passionate you are, though.'

He kisses my face with his cold lips and mutters, 'And your skin is so soft!' he kisses my face some more and says, 'I've never met anyone as intense as you are. It's incredibly exotic!' I'm praying to my non-existent god that he hasn't felt the dampness of my cheeks. It seems he has not.

I disrupt his callous kisses, break his embrace and leave his bed. James asks if I'm going to the loo.

'I'm going home,' The word 'home' sticks in my mouth like stale candy. 'I feel like sleeping in my own bed tonight.'

'Are you okay?' he asks.

'Yes, I'm okay,' I reply, just to shut him up. I know I will palpitate in my bed all night long. And when it's morning in Iran, I will call my mummy like a lost little boy, crying that I want to return to Iran. That everywhere else is hideous. That there are acid attacks in London as well. In Hackney, for instance. *How come you haven't heard about it? How come it isn't on the news?*

'As you like,' James tells me in a frozen tone of voice. 'Let me walk you to the station.'

I ask him not to. I convince him to stay in bed. He's too drunk and sleepy to argue.

I am out again, letting London caress my skin. I find myself thinking of Lubna, of two years ago, when we first met in that half-dark hostel in glamourous Istanbul, both applying for our visas to our utopia called Europe. How young we were! I was twenty-two and she twenty-four. I got accepted as an international student, she did not as an artist who had become a refugee. While embracing her goodbye, she spilled out that she was 'crazy about' me, her English suddenly sounding as deep as Arabic, her large eyes glistening more than usual. I remember I thought she was the most intense person I'd ever met. Not exotic, just intense. And I loathed myself for leaving her, and our love, like I loathed myself for leaving my parents, and our home.

I start to run.

Transit

The Ukrainian waiter is shouting at me in bad English that my bacon sandwich contains bacon. 'You sure you want it? No Halal!'

I feel like answering his idiotic question with another idiotic one: 'Why do you assume I am Muslim and don't eat bacon? Does my fiery red v-neck shirt and loose hair look like hijab to you?'

And then I remember it is my dark features. No matter how much skin and hair I put on display, in the eyes of the airport staff, I will always be one thing: a Muslim.

I hungrily look around at other customers who are all talking in loud Ukrainian, chuckling with the waiters who are suddenly very welcoming. They are all white. The women are skinny and have long, blonde hair, the men are sturdy and have bald heads. The women who push prams look both furious and frustrated. The men all look the same: expressionless. I find most of the boys to be terribly beautiful. They are tall, and have large blue eyes, their smooth skin radiating youth. But their belligerent manners ruin it all. I wish I were in Imam Khomeini airport waiting for my luggage, waving from behind the vast expanse of glass window to my parents.

My *haram* sandwich arrives after half an hour and I assume the waiters have taken turns to spit on my Muslim bacon. Turns out they haven't. In fact, I realise this is the most delicious sandwich I have ever eaten. The bacon tastes so fresh it melts in my mouth and for those few seconds that my sandwich lasts I forget how exhausted I am and I forget about the xenophobic episode. I catch the eye of the waiter but I avoid leaving any tips. Also, I conclude the sausage sandwiches my dad made me for school were even better than the one I just had. Because they were elaborate. Everything was planned and loved before being put inside the baguette, and the mayonnaise was homemade. My dad makes mayonnaise with organic eggs and vinegar and oil. It takes him ages, and the whole family is deafened by the cacophony of his blender, but it is the only mayonnaise I like and ever eat. I decide the constant trips to Tehran, which are messing up my body and mind, are worth it.

After devouring my spectacular sandwich, I check the time. I still have ten more hours to kill in Borispol airport. I want to weep. But this is the price I have to pay for flying cheaply. I have paid 200 quid for a return trip from London to Tehran. Apparently, my grandma declared, 'This is the price of a ticket to fly from Tehran to Kish! This can't be the price of an international flight.' And I know I will boast about this economic accomplishment of mine until the day I die.

For this price, I have to spend eleven hours in a god-forsaken airport where officers look like soldiers carrying shotguns and if you speak English to them, they reply in

Ukrainian, acting offended. Ukrainian sounds like Russian and I love the Russian language, because when I was a teenager, it was my dream to read Pushkin in the original language, but I never got the chance to study it further than the beautiful alphabet. My favourite line from his poetry was, 'loving autumn is like loving a dying girl.' I want to quote this to them, but they look like a bunch of furious supermodels, so I just pretend I understand Ukrainian pretty well.

I did not sleep last night as I started my journey at midnight. From London to Gatwick, and from Gatwick to Ukraine. But my final destination is my family in Iran.

This airport is smaller than Gatwick and Imam Khomeini; one can scrutinise the whole place in less than half an hour. It is sparkling clean and the dominant colour is light grey, apart from fuchsia perfume adverts on the walls. A stereotypically seductive voice is announcing all the flights in Ukrainian in an overbearing volume. I wander about in this claustrophobic space, until I decide to get some sleep on the white plastic chairs. I feel like I am homeless. I have put my trainers as a pillow under my head to give my swollen feet a rest.

I dream I get arrested in Imam Khomeini airport because they find out that I am carrying two packs of smoked bacon in my suitcase – the best British souvenir for my brother.

I wake up and laugh at my ridiculous nightmare. I think of my family and feel tearful. I know even though I was in Iran a few months ago, my parents will look older and so will I. And we will look at each other's new wrinkles, wondering why this should be our life. This constant travelling, missing, transiting, transferring, transforming, and yet never reaching. And this is the tragedy of us: we don't ever conform, we will never belong, no matter where we are. Was that Homi Bhabha who defined people like us 'unhomed and stateless' or another tedious thinker?

I find a smiling man and ask him to watch my luggage. I then escape to Duty Free. It is embarrassingly small for an airport with so many adverts on the walls. After examining every beauty product like a proper scientist, I choose an Artdeco lip gloss. I am pleased because I haven't seen much of Artdeco in London, whereas when I was living in Tehran it was one of my favourite brands. My new lip gloss is the colour of bacon. I give the cashier pounds, but she does not accept them, acting as though I have shown her a snake: she is shouting in Ukrainian, looking both terrified and furious. Her colleague, who looks like less of an impoverished model, rescues me and accepts my debit card, without speaking to me.

Suddenly, I get anxious that the guy who is watching my bag has stolen my rucksack, with all my underwear and the library books I will have to pretend to study in Tehran so my parents won't harass me about not being a hard-working student.

When I reach the chairs, I realise the smiling fat man in stained jeans was actually a trustworthy angel who looked after my luggage well. Therefore, I ask him to continue to watch my bags.

I weave my way to the crowded ladies room, and all I want is to put on my lip gloss. To have bacon lips, instead of real lips, which are chapped, dry, cracked, colourless, and stateless. I look in the monstrous mirrors and I realise even if I buy the whole rack of Artdeco, I won't look human until I get some sleep. In my own bed. In one of my beds. Either the one in London, or the one in Tehran. Or on any bed for that matter, as opposed to sleeping on a plastic chair.

I put on my lip gloss, and can't stop staring in the mirror as I realise I have never looked so strange: I look like a corpse with two rashers of glistening bacon for lips.

I want to talk to my niece, who lives in Canada, in order to make the passage of time less painful. But I need to charge my phone. The plugs don't match. I need to buy a new plug. But in this airport the cheapest one is eighteen pounds. I take out one of my books, but realise I feel anything but poetic at the moment. I pay eighteen quid with a broken heart and purchase a plug from a rude but annoyingly beautiful boy. I imagine pulling down his grey trousers in the bathroom and this thought makes me wet, but his manners are so uncouth that I run back to my plastic chairs, dry and crazed.

I am so bored and aimless that I even consider making friends in the airport. Soon I notice nobody is as much of a loser as me to spend eleven hours in transit. The other passengers are walking swiftly, purposefully, leaving me behind, stuck to my plastic chair.

I socialise with all my family members and friends from all over the world through my phone. But the time just does not flow. I am stuck. And in my frustration and exhaustion I panic that I might get trapped in this diabolical airport for good.

The Ukrainians keep changing our gate. It is now D15, the last exit, downstairs.

When I am in D15, which is a tiny gate with white plastic chairs, I suddenly feel I am already in Iran, as I am surrounded by Iranians. I feel warm and calm. I start a conversation with an older woman who has wrapped herself in leopard print and has dyed her hair orange-blonde. Typical middle-class Iranian housewife. I talk as well to a young woman who is wearing glasses and is flying from Helsinki. I tell them about my eternal transit and they pity me. I quite like them. I like the attention they are giving me. Until the woman in leopard print says in an angry tone, 'Belgium has become full of foreigners: black people, Arabs, all of them. No real Europeans any more. I wonder what's happening to the rest of Europe when this has happened in the kernel of Europe, Brussels.'

'But what is a real European?' I ask without waiting for her response. 'You? For your information, black people have lived in Europe for generations.'

'You obviously don't have a clue!' she yells.

I look at her crooked eyeliner and I am too tired to detest her or fight back. I decide to punish her by staring at the walls behind her and aggressively avoid any eye contact.

As I'm thinking that my life cannot get any worse, a man with a heavily bearded face brings out his musical instrument, a *setar*, and starts playing bad traditional Iranian music for an hour. When he stops, I am on the verge of screaming at the top of my lungs, deafening myself and everyone else in the process. I feel invaded. This was even worse than the leopard print's racist remarks, because this was unpredictable and lengthy. Everybody applauds when he finishes as if this was genuinely a concert and it was good music.

Finally, they open the boarding gate and we are all now in the queue. I join the woman from Helsinki, asking her how she finds living there. I tell her some of my favourite bands are from Finland, and that is the reason why I am aiming to visit it one day. She looks at me as though I were speaking the language of aliens. Her facial expression is empty and she mutters, 'I'm an engineer, Germany would be much better for me, but they need to sort out their governmental issues first and let fewer refugees in if they want an engineer like me. I cannot deal with so many refugees. This is the only problem Finland doesn't have.'

I imagine Finland and Germany at war with each other over the presence of this amazing engineer, each wanting her for themselves, fighting over her, while shooting other immigrants, because that is her order. I know I am hallucinating, I think I should be happy, people take drugs to get to this point, whereas I can feel out of my mind just by trapping myself for eleven hours in transit.

When the irritated supermodels issue us our new boarding passes, we are pushed into a bus in order to get to the aeroplane. These Ukrainian aeroplanes are miniscule, but according to my father, very good and new.

In the bus, I can't find a seat, therefore I stand, throwing my rucksack on the floor as my back is burning with pain. I close my eyes for a second, the bus trembles, and a woman starts screaming,

'Why don't you look at me? Why do Iranians hate each other? Why are you like this? If you look at other nations, nobody behaves like you do. Americans are friends with each other, Arabs are good to each other! Why do you hate each other? It is your own problem!'

Her invasive words get louder, I have opened my eyes, first ironically, then I am in shock. I find it interesting that she is excluding herself from 'Iranians' and is addressing us as 'you'.

205

Nobody says anything, people just give each other uncomfortable smiles, some murmuring, *'Divoonas'*, 'she is crazy'. I catch the eye of a woman with a pale complexion, she is standing at the other side of the bus, in a navy velvet jacket, her hair dark like mine, undyed and curly. We stare at each other with surreptitious smiles, and fortunately the bus stops.

Then I am pushed into the plane. The air hosts and hostesses are surprisingly nice and welcome us with smiles. They have learned to say 'hello' to their international passengers. I find my seat, and after a few seconds, the woman in the velvet jacket comes and sits beside me. I realise that, despite my lack of faith in God, I was praying for this. But the passenger next to her is the racist in leopard print, so God is not completely on my side. I have a window seat, therefore I can stare out at the passing sky and pretend I am alone, and this is my private jet, instead of the cheapest option possible, however, my legs are already smashed in the tightness of the space in my private jet.

It is bedtime in Ukraine, and probably in London and Tehran and everywhere else. Normal people who aren't stateless like me, are in bed now, or brushing their teeth, cleansing their face for a good night's sleep. The woman in velvet touches my shoulder, I avert my eyes from the clouds, and she gives me a bright smile, asking me an irrelevant question. 'Sorry, but do you know the time in Germany?' I am wondering whether to take this as an ice breaker, the opening of an in-flight flirtation, or just a ridiculous question. Either way, I do not know the answer. I apologise, smiling back, saying, 'I don't know,' asking, 'Is that where you're coming from?'

'No,' she replies, 'I'm coming from Sweden. What about

you?' She uses the formal you, *shoma*. Very polite. I like it. She tells me that her name is Niusha and she is doing her masters in theatre studies.

The leopard print is fast asleep. We can hear her snore while we flirt about *Ivanov* and *Hedda Gabler*. I notice that, unlike most other women on the plane, Niusha is not wearing any make-up, yet her lips look soft and smooth. I do not stare at them too much, as I assume she might just be a friendly person who is bored as fuck on this forced endless adventure, and isn't necessarily after a fuck.

Despite the fact that her family also live in Sweden, she regularly travels back to Iran. 'Why?' I ask her, genuinely curious.

'Because I love Iran. It is my most important inspiration,' she informs me. 'No place else is like Iran. Nobody else parties as hard as us.' She laughs and winks at me, which makes me wild. I take out my new lip gloss and reapply it, trying to look confident, even imperious. I find her staring at my lips. Mission accomplished. I smile at her with my shiny, plumped up lips, 'so where in Iran do you live?'

I am almost certain she is from Tehran, and I am already thinking of excuses to ditch our torturous family gatherings in order to hang out with her. I can imagine her living in a posh place like Zaferanieh. We can hang out in their private pool and her younger brother will cook Persian cuisine for us, which is the thing I miss the most in London. I will encourage her brother to cook me a nice *fesenjoon*. I shall bring the fresh walnuts from my grandmother's garden.

However, she destroys my dreams by informing me she is going to stay in her hometown, Shiraz, in her uncle's house. And she is an only child. 'But come and visit.'

'Sure,' I say, already knowing another trip and I will die. I never travel if I don't have to, this is the lesson I have learned from living between two continents. From being always on the move, always in transit, never arriving.

'So do you go to many theatres when you're in Iran? There are so many new plays at the moment.'

'Last summer I went to see the Iranian adaptation of *Ivanov* in Teatre Shahr, however–' suddenly her sentence gets broken by screams filling the airplane like gas, and I am frightened, thinking the plane is being shot at by Putin. Then I realise it is two women literally fighting at the back of the plane, one of them shouting, 'get your hands off me, you idiot!' The leopard print racist wakes up, excitedly looking back, and asking us whether a woman has been molested by a man. 'No.' Niusha replies, as I am still punishing leopard print by not acknowledging her existence. Although I am not certain whether or not she has noticed she is being punished.

It is the same voice from the bus screaming back, 'I did not touch you, you yourself are crazy!'

An air steward runs down the aisle towards the back of the plane, I am dying to know what is going on. We all are. All the Iranian passengers look excited – ecstatic even. I do not mean to generalise, but we Iranians relish being the voyeurs of a proper public fight. The Ukrainians, on the other hand, seem distressed.

Niusha and I look at each other, and I know my eyes are as wide as hers. We are both on the verge of hysterical laughter.

Leopard print cannot tolerate the suspense and actually leaves her seat to see what is going on. By now, a Ukrainian steward has changed the seat of one of the women, who accused the other woman of pulling her hair. Leopard print returns to her seat with hands filled with news: 'apparently, the crazy woman who ranted on the bus about Iranians was ranting again, and this other woman asked her whether she has taken her pills, so the crazy woman attacked her.' But as the leopard print's thrill withers away, her facial expression turns into mournful fury, and she declares, 'Oh my God! They are making us lose face in front of Ukrainians . . .'

Niusha and I act as though we are deaf, staring at the back of the seats in front of us. What I really want at the moment is to see the physical appearance of the ranting woman, because so far I have only heard her. But I am also too frightened to get close to her. As usual, my fear defeats my curiosity. She is so unstable that her passport has been confiscated.

After this rush of adrenalin, I find it impossible to sleep. Niusha is pretending to be asleep. They have turned off the lights, and still I can see her long neck, shining, a beacon in the dark. I am staring at it shamelessly, I want her to stop pretending that she is asleep. To open her eyes. To look at me again, attentive, assertive, and willing.

I look at the dark clouds outside my window; I remember when I was a child, I always imagined the clouds being scoops of ice cream, and I did not want to lick them, I just wanted to walk on them and feel their tender coldness. I am also feeling sleepy; I stop staring at the clouds and look away from the window, finding Niusha gazing at me, her dark eyes wide awake, her lips unsmiling and open. Our faces are stuck together for only a second. I can feel her licking off my bacon lip gloss, but in an instant there's a loud Russian announcement on the plane and the lights are on – we stop, scared, looking at leopard print. She was asleep, but now opens her bloodshot eyes to ask us, 'how long?' I want her to die.

The plane is speeding up while landing. The pace is exciting me, until it stops. I transfer my red, knitted scarf from my neck to my head. There is a Ukrainian announcement, and then an English one that sounds like Ukrainian, informing us we have arrived in Iran. People applaud. Niusha and I avoid each other's eyes. Leopard print takes out an orange, satin scarf from her golden plastic bag, and throws it on her head. 'Welcome to the land of mullahs!' She says, addressing Niusha and me, waiting for us to burst out laughing at her unoriginal, over-used joke. I take my final revenge by staring into her eyes, trying my best to look like a frozen stone. Niusha is nice, because she smiles at her while putting a black *shal* over her voluptuous curls. I think I succeed, because leopard print fucks off without saying anything more to us. Niusha and I follow each other on Instagram so that we can hang out if she comes to London or Tehran, or if I go to Stockholm or Shiraz, but I know we will never see each other again.

The Imam Khomeini airport is so bright and crowded that it does not feel like three hours after midnight. While waiting for my suitcase to arrive on the luggage belt, I gallop towards the extensive window that is now the only barrier between me and my family. I have passed so many borders; I am exhausted but ecstatic. I see my mother waving at me energetically as though it is three in the afternoon, not 3 a.m. And then I see my father also waving and laughing, his artificial teeth as shiny and beautiful as the moon. I am getting emotional, as though this is my first time travelling back to Iran. I blow them a kiss and point at the conveyor-belt that is going around with the suitcases of the passengers. I get a glimpse of Niusha, who has found her tiny red suitcase, and we conveniently ignore each other.

As always, my suitcase is the last to arrive.

Glossary

Azad: Expensive universities in Iran that are relatively easy to get in, offering more accessible education mostly for candidates who cannot get accepted by *sarasari* universities

Azizam: Farsi word meaning my dear

Bad hejab: In Iran this is a term applied to women whose hijab is not chaste enough

Divooneh: Equivalent of crazy in spoken Farsi

Faranseh: Farsi for France

Fenjan: Farsi term meaning an elegant delicate cup for tea and Turkish coffee

Hamjensbaz: A derogatory term for homosexual

Heyvoon: Animal in colloquial Farsi. Also, a common insult to describe people with aggressive or bad manners

Hezbollahi: Islamist

Manteau: A word of French origin meaning cloak or overcoat, used in Iran to indicate the jacket women wear as part of their *hejab*

Namahram: An Islamic term describing a man and a woman who are not bound to each other by either blood or marriage.

Nazr: Praying to a sacred figure to grant one's wish, and once the wish is granted, one visits the sacred figure's shrine or does a good deed, for instance giving money to the poor

Ommol: A colloquial pejorative in contemporary Farsi to describe narrow-minded people who lack sophisticated manners

Salamati: Farsi for health

Sarasari: Free universities in Iran that are state-funded and require passing a difficult competitive nation-wide exam, *konkoor,* to get in as they offer a high-quality education

Sharab: Farsi for wine

Shomal: North in colloquial Farsi, it is often used to convey The North of Iran, which is a common holiday destination

Soosool: A derogatory term in colloquial Farsi to describe young fussy people

Shal: Farsi word for shawl

Tavaledet Mobarak: Farsi for Happy Birthday to you!

Viroos: Farsi term meaning virus

Yaoi: a Japanese term meaning anime erotica with the theme of same-sex love and desire between boys

Acknowledgements

Tehran Yaoi was first published in The Mechanics' Institute Review Issue 15 in 2018. And *Soho* was first published, under a different title, *Choke* in The Mechanics' Institute Review Issue 14 in 2017 under my then pseudonym, Sogol Sur.

This book wouldn't have existed without the inspiration and assistance of Julia Bell, Rebecca Carter, Matthew Bates, Morteza N, Marina Warner, Honor Gavin, Sue Tyley, Hilary Key, Sarah Beal, Kate Beal, Keith Jarrett, Mehdi Khan Ahmadi, Sheida Mousavi, and my fabulous father.